Asma Alzarouni

Killing Me Once more

Asma Alzarouni is a UAE writer and novelist born in Sharjah. She holds a Bachelor of Education degree. She is affiliated with several literary organizations, including the Emirates Writers Union (vice president) and the Emirates Female Writers Association (a founding member). She has published more than seventeen books in the field of literature, including several novels and collections of short stories.

Killing Me Once More

A Novel by
Asma Alzarouni

Translated by
Abdallah Altaiyeb

Strategic Book Publishing and Rights Co.

Strategic Book Publishing & Rights Co., LLC
USA | Singapore
www.sbpra.net

For information about special discounts for bulk purchases, please contact Strategic Book Publishing and Rights Co. Special Sales, at bookorder@sbpra.net.

ISBN: 978-1-68181-706-4

Dedication

You were in my thoughts the moment I wrote my first word. Since then, my writing flowed seamlessly, running apace with my heartbeat whenever your image pulsed in my head. Ask the nights, dark as they were, for they befriended me. The distance tortured me, bringing tears to my eyes and pouring pain into my words, as I recalled the sound of your voice in my mind.

Writing this bittersweet dedication—gifting someone with the agony of words—was hard, and I struggled with my feelings, for the names of many came rushing to my memory: childhood comrades, writing friends, authors, intellectuals, inspiring personalities.

To you all, my friends, as well as writers and intellectuals around the world who are hoping to build global cultural bridges through literature, I dedicate this book, a journey of love bounded by an astonishing loyalty.

Asma Alzarouni

Foreword

I'm a reasonably well-educated American—a retired library director as well as a writer and editor. I've handled manuscripts by writers from all over the world. Yet when I received a passionately romantic book from a woman in the United Arab Emirates, I was very surprised.

I didn't know Emirati women wrote love stories.

In my defense, most Americans know very little about the Arab world. Much of what we think we know is wrong. I thought, for example, that Arab men went around in billowing white robes and headscarves, conducting their society's business. I did not know that Arab women went around at all—I thought most of them merely bustled through the markets, virtually illiterate, covered from head to foot in garments they did not want to wear.

Needless to say, these ideas have little basis in fact. But I believed them, so when I received the manuscript of Asma Alzarouni's *Killing Me Once More*, I was baffled. The author is obviously educated. Her female protagonist Nora drives a car, uses a cell phone, went to college, has a job, is much more fluent in social media than I am, yet wears an abaya with pride. Most astonishing of all, Nora is married but in love with another man.

Asma Alzarouni's Nora is a twenty-first-century Emirati with hopes and dreams, passions and regrets. Twenty-six years ago, Alzarouni tells us, Nora was a single college student. When she met a handsome Kuwaiti in the lobby of a hotel frequented by students, it was love at first sight. Unfortunately, marriages in the United Arab Emirates were—and still are—arranged by parents, and there was no way Nora's parents would ever condone a marriage between their beloved, talented daughter and an unknown Kuwaiti poet they'd never even met. She had already been promised to a distant cousin, which was the custom in their family. It was, as they say in the States, a done deal.

Desperate, Nora sought advice from a friend who actually did marry for love. Samira advised her to back down and marry the man her parents chose for her; to do otherwise would ostracize her from the family, as had happened to Samira. That would be just too hard. Nora took Samira's advice and married Eisa, bearing him two children a few years later.

But not a day went by that she did not think of the poet in Alexandria, and wonder if she'd made a mistake. Back in the twentieth century, when long-distance connections within the Arab world were tenuous, there seemed little chance that Nora's questions would ever be more than musings. But then came Facebook, Twitter, and WhatsApp, and suddenly people who had been out of touch for a quarter of a century could be right at the tip of one's finger.

Killing Me Once More is very much a novel of the twenty-first century; indeed, it could not take place at any other time. It is also a novel of tensions—between old traditions and new technology, between a patriarchal culture and cosmopolitan women.

Unquestionably Nora's emotions are very muddled. At one point she moans, "I . . . have been searching for my heart, only to find that it has fallen into a well, trying to breathe the whispers of passion, feeling abandoned by the one who ripped it from my body and continued on his way, not looking back once." When at last her renewed relationship with her lover manages to go beyond the texting stage, translator Abdullah Altaiyeb beautifully renders the scene:

"As [Nora] turned her head to cross the street, she gasped in surprise and the mobile phone fell from her hand. There he was, standing right in front of her! She found herself looking at him as she never had before, noting how the years had touched him. She knew she had changed over the years as well, and was no longer the girl he had last seen a quarter of a century ago. The encounter made her speechless, the words she wished to say to him hung on the tip of her tongue, but not a word escaped her lips. He too was wordless, staring at her face.

. . . A long, silent moment passed between them, broken when her mobile phone rang."

Killing Me Once More does not offer easy solutions, because there are none. But Asma Alzarouni offers a clear-eyed look at a culture in transition and the collateral damage that occurs along the way.

In the Gulf, where only a handful of novels are published annually, the road to print isn't easy. Nonetheless, Alzarouni is the author of a significant body of work; this particular novel was published in Arabic in 2015 in Kuwait. She subsequently met a wonderful friend and translator, Abdallah Altaiyeb, who prepared this English translation. It's not a literal translation from the Arabic, nor should it be. It turns colloquial Arabic into eminently readable and engaging English, and in the process bring Nora to life for the English-speaking reader. The Arabic edition held up a mirror to allow Arab women to see themselves in Nora; Altaiyeb holds up a pair of spectacles to allow English-speaking readers to see the world through Nora's eyes.

Killing Me Once More will introduce readers of English to an Arab point of view they know too little about. At the same time, it blasts apart many stereotypes we have held much too long. We are part of a global community, and our planet teems with people who do not speak like us, do not dress like us, whose customs are very different. But when we read books written by people of different cultures, we learn we're not that different after all.

I am aware that some of Asma Alzarouni's works have already been anthologized in English. But I am very proud to have had a hand, however small, in introducing her to a wider audience in the English-speaking world.

Karen Bernardo
Editor, writer, novelist, and retired library director
Author of *The Perfect Spin of a Rifle*, *The Perfect Cake for a Lady*, and *The Perfect Saint has a Secret*

Author's Preface

When I dream of my childhood, I am running down the silvery beach that lies behind my father's shop, racing with time to catch one final glimpse of the sun before it disappears under the wavy surface of the ocean. My friends and I would scrawl large letters on the sands, celebrating their beauty while it lasted, before the tide dragged them into the bottomless sea. My biggest fear was that the sun would be abducted by the sea, for my grandmother had told me tales of men who had vanished in its depths during the pearl-fishing seasons.

I loved the sea, but hated its surging waves; they scared me the most. I often went running into the arms of my father, asking him why the sea always ran after our sun. He would caress my head and tousle my hair with affection, saying, "My little darling, the sun will only be away for few hours and will be back before you know it. Do you know why it leaves us? So that you can get some sleep and make sweet dreams that you will eventually weave into a beautiful reality."

The gulls flapped and circled above my head, squawking a message to humanity, while I indulged in building castles in the sands. It was there on the beach that I first had a vision of my dream and began pursuing it, making it come true. The first letters I scribbled on the sands with my little fingers became words and then messages to the people of my community as I tried to live their joys and share their sorrows. My first book saw the light in 1994, a collection of short stories entitled *Whispering Beaches*. Soon after, my dream grew bigger and I grew with it—within the bounds of books, in the folds of newspapers, and in various media outlets. I wrote articles and feature stories, and attended intellectual symposia.

My dream kept on growing; by then I had authored and published more than twenty-five books, ranging from novels and short stories to children's books and free verse. Still, my dream kept growing stronger and broader—a dream to reach with my words a wider world, from one country to another, from one language to another, through the art of translation. Eventually, my novel *The Court's Drive* was translated into several languages, including French, Portuguese, Indian, Italian, and Russian.

Yet it was English, the global language, that I was after, and I saved this honor for my dearest novel, *Killing Me Once More*, which I had written while I accompanied my son for medical treatment in the United Kingdom. It all started with a phone call from a friend, telling me details of her love story, parts of which she had already shared with me a long time ago. The idea of expanding her story, turning it into a novel, came naturally to my mind, and so, through the power of a writer's imagination, I started forming the words and assembling the sentences.

Meeting Abdallah Altaiyeb, a renowned writer and translator, on social media was a stroke of good fortune that triggered my ultimate dream of dreams: to reach with my words, on the wings of the English language, limitless grounds and countless readers. Now, with this brilliant translation, I am looking forward to seeing my novel span the whole of Europe, North America, and, as a matter of fact, the whole world, sharing our beautiful Arabic culture, with love, through words— thereby enriching the culture of its readers.

We have spent a great deal of our lives reading translated Western writings, yet we did not, could not, reciprocate the favor and gratify the West with our own contribution, for the number of translated Arabic books was insignificant; it still is. The burden now lies on us to put more effort towards complementing the world's literature with our own, affirming the strong presence of our creative writings. I hope my novel will contribute to this effort and appeal to readers all over the world, inspiring them to explore Arabic literature and culture. To this end, I have full trust in the great work of the publisher, SBPRA.

Asma Alzarouni
Emirati poet, novelist, and educator
December 2019

(1)

Whenever she recalled those memories, Nora would smile, but her eyes would show indescribable sadness and pain, the vision of his face still vivid in her mind. The dream of meeting him again never left her, haunting her every day, leaving her wondering what he would look like now. Had the years taken their toll on him? Would he still remember her as she remembered him? Would he recognize her, if ever they happened to meet again?

Her mobile phone buzzed, its alert tone reminding her of the date and time; it was noon on July seventh. Casting a look at the calendar on the wall of her room, she hastily grabbed a pen from the top of the desk and drew a circle around the date on the calendar, mentally counting the past years in which she had circled the same date. She was still the same spirited person, smiling joyfully at any passing memory, ready to be swept away by his captivating image whenever it appeared in her mind.

Snapped out of her memories and into reality by the sound of approaching footsteps, she wiped a tear from her cheek and left her room, closing the door behind her.

In the hall, her daughter, Alia, cheerily grabbed her hand. “Did you forget we were going shopping for my wedding dress? Are you ready to go?”

The mother gazed at her daughter’s face and realized how fast she had grown. She passed a hand over the girl’s head, quietly pulling her into a hug. “How could I forget? Let’s be off.”

Deep inside, she was thinking of a way to memorialize this very special day in the calendar of her heart. Even though she had a busy life as a writer and lecturer, she always set aside a fixed time of day to be alone with her memories of him. Alia had interrupted her solitude—but of course Alia’s needs were important too. Were they more important than her own?

On their way to the fashion stores, the young girl was very chatty, surfing the internet on her mobile phone, browsing through the images in search of the perfect wedding dress design. Nora slipped into daydreaming, her eyes scanning the congested streets of Sharjah as she drove.

“Mom, stop here!” Alia shouted suddenly. “I want to go to that shop! My friend Abeer is waiting for me there.”

Nora reversed the car to the shop that she’d just driven by without noticing it. “Go ahead, then. I’ve got to run a quick errand, but I’ll come back to you soon.”

Getting the permission of her daughter, she drove away to be alone with his image in her mind, to eternalize his memory, far from the noisiness and worries of the present day.

There was one place she used to go to reminisce about her lost love. She wanted to go there again, to retreat into her own mind, relive their first encounter and sail deep into her memories of the first time their eyes made contact. It had been twenty-six years since then. A misty goodbye moment, lacking necessary details, left a vacancy inside her heart, for he gave her no chance to take one last glimpse of his eyes. Nor did he give her time to bid him adieu and throw herself on him, sobbing, pleading, and begging him not to leave. His cruel decision to walk out on her with no justification or excuses that would otherwise lessen the weight of her agony, had caused her to live her life halfheartedly with broken dreams ever since. A stray wish, a few passing encounters, and some vivid scenes in the past had taken control of her life, as if her memory could only keep the details of that particular period of time; the clock seemed to have stopped eternally there, and her memory space had all been occupied with those past images, refusing to take in more.

The memories of the university, the beach, and the saltiness of the sea often mixed with her tears, forming a tapestry of torture that was all part of that period. That day in July, the summer of 1989, refused to be forgotten; it was etched on her memory with all of its finest details.

She had never been on a date before. She had never known the meaning of shivering from anything but fear; she had never experienced such a feeling before, so she was certainly not able to classify it.

On her first day in Alexandria, she had gone to el-Haram Hotel with her brother Jamal to check in; this was the favorite residence for Gulf students attending the university or taking exams there. As she prepared to hand her passport to the hotel receptionist, she dropped it on the floor. It was suddenly scooped up and returned to her by a man so handsome he took her breath away. Astonished, she stared at him. A strange feeling engrossed her, a blend of anxiety and wonder; she almost lost her balance, as she was too young to handle the situation and too inexperienced to come to grips with what was happening to her at that moment. She did nothing in the face of the situation, only stared at him helplessly with an innocent, childlike smile. His gaze overwhelmed her heart, assuming full control over it, and the memory of it had held her captive to the present day. It was just a mere look, yet it was so deep and full of meaning that it became impossible for her to forget it.

From that moment on, she had to fence her heart behind bars of concealment, burying the secret of love within its layers. Nonetheless, he began to grow inside her like a baby, getting stronger and stronger with time; she was afraid that one day it would show and expose her—as if she were at fault! Every day, she would steal an hour for herself to be alone with him, to ask him why, to reprimand him one second and hold him tight the next, to take refuge in him like a dream, running away from the pain and disappointment of reality.

Today, putting Alia and her wedding plans aside, Nora drove her car to the sea. She had no friends but the sea, and no one knew her whole secret other than the sea. She stared at the Arabian Gulf, stretching its blue color to the horizon, and drew her words on its sands, spreading her pain among the waves, sending him yearning messages. She imagined that somehow they would reveal themselves to her lover standing on the opposite bank. She was certain that this sea, with its mightiness, was the only thing standing between them. It seemed, to her mind, as if the sea was a transparent barrier that could easily be crossed, and she told herself that a meeting with him was possible one day. The fact that she was married, the mother of a young woman about to become a bride and a son about to graduate from college, had no reality.

She had been obsessed with reading love stories, poems, and romance novels since the first and only time she fell in love. One of her favorites was "Alatlal," the poem by Ibrahim Nagi, which had been recorded as a popular song by Um Kulthum. Since Ibrahim Nagi had managed to meet his childhood sweetheart, it was only fair that fate would arrange a date for her with her lover at a time of revelation. On this day of all days, that strange feeling returned to her.

Something was surging frantically in her tired veins; her imagination was confused. She tended to echo the feelings in every love story that came her way, trying to recapture the love that had nestled inside her. She wondered what her romance would be like if it were allowed to blossom and grow. Would her life, one day, turn into a love story like Qays and Laila, or Antara and Abla, or even Romeo and Juliet? In the end, her tale had something that distinguished it from theirs. She would earn herself a special place in the history of lovers.

She stood up, brushed the sand from her dress, and reluctantly returned to the car. It was time to meet Alia at the shop.

Nora went through the rest of the evening on autopilot. Her husband, Eisa, was away on business. She switched off the lights and drew the curtain of the window, hoping to block the door of memory. Tossing and turning on her bed, the same thoughts cycled over and over again; as she covered her face with a small pillow, she forcefully declared the end of all of her thinking. But it was no use. Hours later, she saw the first light of dawn approaching, leading to a hard day ahead.

It was Tuesday. She came down with dull and sluggish steps and sat with her family. Picking up her mobile phone, she scanned for new messages and posts in the virtual world that sheltered her words, like a haven for her heart that was fastened to the unknown.

Sagged into the comfort of the couch, she calmly sipped her coffee, dipping into its bubbles, looking casually at the screen of her phone. The next thing she knew, a new tweet violently shook her body; she read it over and over again to regain control over herself. She read the tweet as if she were reading herself.

> "Take me as words among those you wrote whenever the world closed in on you in spite of its vastness, take me as your unhappiness which you have suppressed, or tears you have shed in a moment of sadness."

Take me as. . . take me as. . . She read those words times without number. Even though this kind of tweet reached her, on a daily basis, dozens of times from her two thousand followers, this particular message confused her. Who could have sent it? She held the phone in her hand, waiting for more messages. Finally, a call came.

"Hello, who's speaking?" she answered quickly.

"You're Nora. You studied with me at the university in Alexandria, twenty-six years ago," said a familiar voice.

Her heart pounded, for the voice was captivating. She was silent for a long time, her memory tape suddenly rewinding back to their first encounter. She then became aware of her children sitting next to her, so she sneaked out with her phone, getting a little away from them.

Summoning her strength, she answered with a husky voice, "Yes, I am—I am—Nora."

The line went dead. She tried to call back, but the caller's number appeared to be hidden. Terrified, she waited, eyes darting to the phone screen all day, hoping he would call back. Whenever her phone rang, she would jump and answer.

Could it really be conceivable that he was back? Was he the vision that accompanied me all my life? Showing up now? But why now, and how? To ask me, "Are you Nora?"

Yet, in the interminable hours of her solitude, she answered him back.

Yes, my heart and my love; I am the remnant of Nora, the one with a stolen spirit, living my life, a body without a soul.

(2)

The hours dragged on and her day passed long. Nothing occupied Nora but the screen of her mobile phone, while the messages of her friends piled up on social media, unread. She kept looking at the images of the account holder who had charmed her with his words and pierced the contents of her soul. She contemplated the obscure images, nothing appearing on his account but an image of a watch on a man's wrist and another image showing part of a man's shoulder, wearing a traditional thobe—the traditional long-sleeved, ankle-length garment worn by men in the Arabian Peninsula. In trying to put together the fragmented images, she became addicted to his page, checking its new contents dozens of times throughout the day.

She tossed and turned in her bed all night, showering the pillow with black rain blended with the bleeding of her heart, asking herself whether this could be possible. Was she awake or lost in a dream? In the early hours before dawn, she grabbed her phone, scrolling down all the numbers, thinking of calling her friends, but how could she tell them her story? She then remembered her friend Salma; she was the only one who knew all of those details. Quickly she texted her friend, asking Salma to meet her at their favorite café at four p.m.

She already thought she knew what Salma would say. For years Salma had accused her of madness, urging her to forget him. "What love are you talking about, Nora? What kind of fidelity runs through your veins? What type of clay were you created from? Whenever we meet in restaurants, you insist on keeping an empty chair next to you, eating while imagining him sitting on it, the man who lied to you, even about his real name, choosing to impersonate a famous poet instead! In those days we didn't have Google to look him up, so back then he could get away with those lies! Remember when you used to buy all those magazines of traditional poetry? I will never forget that day when I showed you the picture of the poet Hamoud on the cover of a Kuwaiti magazine! You snatched the magazine, casting it aside, insisting that the pictures must have been mixed unintentionally. We then went to the bookstore and found a book of Hamoud's verses, and we saw the true Hamoud's picture on the back cover. You could have drowned me in your tears."

Was he playing with my feelings? she thought. *Was I nothing more than mere entertainment to him? I could not convince myself except with love, looking hard for excuses to justify the picture I had painted of him in my imagination. At that time, experience had not jaded my life yet, so I was very sure that it was true love. We had met each other abroad and we had shared the most beautiful moments of our lives; we had dreamt of having a roof sheltering us together; we had built dreams, but we had built them in our imagination!*

Another message came, and she gave it all her attention. "Loneliness is not to be alone but to leave the one you love." A second wave of torment swept through her body at that moment. Were such messages enough to bring her joy? Millions of questions tortured her and she needed satisfactory answers, but of what use would those answers be to her? How would he justify his position? Would he understand the meaning of the words of the song she used to croon whenever she longed for him: "I'll appeal to the Lord of heaven against you every time my eyes tear up; I'll tell my tears of fidelity that only a new love would make me forget"—but had anyone else made her forget? This question had been haunting her for years.

Nora drove to the cafe, chose a table by the window and ordered a coffee. Her gaze fell aimlessly on a magazine cover depicting a group of children playing in a schoolyard. Her thoughts drifted back to her childhood, the days before she fell in love.

She remembered the street where her school stood, and in that neighborhood—the Sheikh's district—was their house. She was born with a sliver spoon in her mouth in a big house, a house full of residents—family, domestic servants, and others, including Pakistanis and other people from the island across the Arabian Gulf. She was her father's petted daughter, and he spared nothing to keep her happy. She could never forget the time the math teacher hit her hand with a ruler so hard that blood ran down. Back in the house, Nora tried to hide her red hand from her father's eyes, but he caught her—red-handed, so to speak.

"Who did this to you? Tell me!" said her father.

May God have mercy on you, Father; you have no idea how many times I have been under the whip of a man who wanted to prove his manhood by beating his wife. And because I was your daughter, I patiently withstood all of that, so you would not be hurt or saddened by my pain and suffering.

I wished my father would have slapped me, waking me up; but he never did, even when my mother complained to him about my frequent afternoon outings to the seashore with our neighbor's daughter. He waved his walking stick in my face, pretending to threaten me just so my mother would hold her peace. My grandmother participated in the event, blaming my father for not naming me Ushba.

"Where did you come up with the name, Nora? It's because of this name that she is a really naughty girl," she said.

I then ran to my father's open arms, sobbing. "I don't want to be called Ushba! Why would I want the name of an herb? I like my name and it's beautiful."

"You're the light of my life," my father said, caressing my head with all the tenderness in the world.

My mother rushed towards him, screaming in his face. "You should be scolding her instead of spoiling her! What if the sea drowned her while we were asleep? She leaves the house at the time of siesta, going swimming in the sea with the neighbor's daughter."

"Don't you worry about her—she is the daughter of the sea; she knows all of its secrets!" said my father.

"You're encouraging her!" My mother was furious.

My father, once more, took notice of my swollen hand from the teacher's beating. "Tomorrow, I shall come to your school. I shall teach your teacher a lesson that she'll never forget—how could she strike you this way?"

"I want a color TV, Father. I want to be the first in our neighborhood to have one." I took advantage of the opportunity, while seeking refuge in his lap.

"I'll bring it to you tomorrow."

"Your mollycoddling will spoil her," my mother screamed. All the same, I kissed my father's forehead.

Nora's mobile rang in her hand, rousing her from a beautiful memory. *Oh, how I wish to be a child again, to throw myself in my loving father's lap one more time!*

"Ugh," she groaned, rolling her eyes. *It's that annoying journalist again; he asks one question, expecting back an answer of several pages! Even the press has no decency these days.*

"Yes, Mr. Murad?"

"Mrs. Nora, my apologies for the inconvenience," the journalist said. "I have an urgent deadline and I hoped you could write me an article, about 500 words. It would be highly appreciated."

She grumbled as he had just roused her from a beautiful reverie, whining to herself that the press only asked the questions, leaving the difficult task of writing the answers to her.

Watching the sunset for a little while, Nora decided that Salma was not coming that day. She texted her a WhatsApp message: "Salma, you're late—I am leaving." Comments and messages on her Facebook page, new Twitter posts and interactions, dozens of messages from WhatsApp groups, and emails from work and readers of her daily column in the local newspaper all crowded together in her phone's memory. Her own memory was occupied with a voice from the past, a hidden phone number, and an obscure Twitter account. She reluctantly picked up her bag and left the café, wishing she didn't have to go home.

She kept a lot of words buried deep inside, for they were difficult to share with anyone. As she entered the house, she met her daughter Alia in the hall.

"Mom, where have you been all day? You know that I need you to help with my wedding."

"Sorry, I have been busy with work. Please forgive me. There's nothing more precious than you, Alia."

"Is it really just work?" Alia asked. "Or has Dad bothered you with something again?"

"No, my love, it's nothing worth talking about. It's just the usual troubles of work. Although I'm also thinking of my life when you leave with your husband after your wedding. I'll be missing you a lot—you're the only one who understands me, Alia. And you're the only one who can weave words into spells, just like me."

Alia hugged her. "I will never leave you! You're the most precious and dear mother a girl could ever have."

At the sound of her phone ringing, she eased out of her daughter's embrace. Seeing that the caller was her husband, her face changed into its typical look of annoyance and she did not answer.

Alia took notice of what had happened. "Who called, Mom? Are you waiting for someone?" she asked her.

"No, no," Nora quickly replied. "You know how annoying the journalists are! I'll go and take a shower—I'm a little tired. You go ahead and eat. I have already eaten outside."

Alia looked a little surprised, but went back to watching television. Nora started up the stairs, feeling the worries of the whole world on her shoulders. She needed to confide in someone; but in whom could she place confidence, and where would she start? She needed to get out everything that had been growing inside her; and besides, those mysterious symbols needed decoding, a solution, an opinion, or simply a discussion. She was used to listening to other people and solving their problems. But she was very discreet about her own, because she was well aware that her status, social position, work, husband, and children would not permit her to fall in love with someone, or even think about the idea. Would it be possible for her now, at her age, to again experience a passionate love and romantic dates, to suffer longing and wish for communion?

Tired of the thoughts that were besieging her, she tried to awaken her voice of reason, thinking that she must forget the issue, part ways with those virtual worlds, and keep away from the messages that took her back to a past that had long since ceased to exist and would never come alive again.

She grabbed her phone to hide her social media accounts, only to see that a friend of hers posted a question: "To literary writers and poets, does love ever die? I want a sincere and candid answer from you."

She quieted a little, deeply thinking. *Should I answer this leading question? Why today? You're torturing me with your question, my friend!*

"Love feeds on our souls, to live eternally, while we die every moment," she posted as her response.

Comments on her post came successively without interruption. Her friend Almaddah copied her post to his Twitter page under her name. More comments flowed and the post was retweeted by many of his massively numerous followers, including the one with the obscure picture.

She continued tracking the post and its repercussions as she could not yet find the courage to close the internet pages. Her time was consumed by flipping through some books of fiction and poetry recently given to her by friends, and following posts and interactions on the pages of social media sites. Time passed; midnight was approaching fast and the day was soon to expire. Once again, the foreseeable future carried no news of a possible rendezvous. A message popped up on her WhatsApp account, but it was from her friend Salma.

"I am sorry, Nora. I was in a meeting, followed by a business dinner party for important guests. I forgot my phone was on silent mode. I just lost track of time."

Nora texted her back. "I need you, Salma—something strange is happening with me."

"What is it? You've got me worried!" Salma wrote back immediately.

"We need to meet tomorrow, Salma," she wrote. "I want to talk to you face to face."

"Fine, we will meet at the café on the lake at six p.m.," Salma confirmed.

Her phone rang exactly a minute before midnight, another hidden number.

"Hello, who is it?" she answered hurriedly.

"It's your love from a quarter of a century ago," said the familiar voice on the other end.

Her heart lurched, pounding wildly. "Who are you? What's your name?"

"How I've longed to hear your voice, still as warm as I ever knew it!"

"Who are you, please?" She recognized his voice, but needed a name to attach to it.

"Happy New Year—another year with you in my heart, Nora," said the voice. The line broke and the connection was lost.

"Hello? *Hello?*" Tormented and traumatized, Nora tightened her grip on the phone under the siege of the shock. *Why does he do that to me?*

(3)

Nora slept badly and was awake at dawn. The first thing she did was text her friend.

"Don't forget, Salma—don't be late for our date."

Then she turned back to her social media accounts. On the home page of the mysterious caller, a new post was featured. "Your voice, coming from behind the clouds, spilled fire on an old wound."

She read the phrase time and time again, diving deeper into its meaning each time; it sounded as if it were speaking of her. Her phone rang and she snatched it up.

"Hello? Who are you? Please be kind to me and tell me who you are," she said.

"Nora, what's the matter with you?" her husband snapped. "It's Eisa. I called you several times last night and you didn't answer. I'm now at Delhi Airport—I'll arrive at Dubai International at seven a.m. So send me the driver. What's wrong with you, anyway?"

She got flustered. "Nothing at all. You know that I don't like to answer unknown callers, Abu Khalid." (A common nickname in Arabic is formed by adding "Abu"—father of—or "Um"—mother of—to the name of the eldest son.)

"My number was hidden?" Eisa asked. "That's very strange. All right, I'll see you tonight."

"You be safe," she told him.

Nora ended the call, her eyes flicking back to her social media accounts, checking to see if there were new posts or messages from her mysterious knight. There was a new image of someone with his back to the camera, draped in the flag of Kuwait. Whispering, "How much I love Kuwait," she posted a comment on the picture.

"My warm regards to Kuwait, my heart."

Drowsiness crept over her as she waited for him to respond. The door opened, waking her up; it was her husband Eisa, standing beside her. He held her phone in his hand and she sat up, terrified.

"What time is it?" she asked, snatching the phone from his hand. "Why didn't you knock on the door?"

"Um Khalid, I just came to see you before I go to my room and sleep. I am extremely tired from traveling—I haven't slept since yesterday," he said.

"Well, thank Allah you're back safe," she murmured, pretending to sound drowsy so he would leave her alone. When he had left the room, she looked through her phone, hoping to find a new comment, but there was nothing. She felt sad, but deep inside she was hoping he was all right. Now that he had come back into her life, she couldn't bear the thought of losing him.

The phone rang, and she jumped. Seeing it was Salma, she answered it right away.

"Five calls from you—what's wrong? Are you okay?" Salma sounded totally bewildered.

"I can't tell you over the phone, Salma. We have to meet today for lunch at Shababeek Restaurant in Alqasba. Come alone—I don't want you to have anyone with you. We need to have an intimate talk—you're my best friend and secret keeper. Don't worry, Salma, it's an old issue that I want to have your opinion about."

Nora wondered whether Salma would support her or stand against her heart. Yet she had no one else to talk with, so she had to confide in her.

"What's the matter?" asked Salma, sounding worried.

"Don't be afraid. I just need to talk to you, that's all. Shall I come and pick you up?"

"No, Nora, you go ahead and I will meet you there," Salma returned.

"Just don't be late—I know you! You'll be the last to leave the office, even though you're the manager! You follow all the traffic rules because you're not crazy like me. Please, please be there by three o'clock—I know you get out of work at 2:30."

Nora washed and dressed quickly, then got in her car at 1 p.m. Since she had time, she decided to pass by the places she loved most in her old neighborhood, which all had given way to new skyscrapers and high-rise buildings. Her middle school had become a hardware market, frequented by Asian visitors. She made a point to take the beach road where she could get rejuvenated by the sight of the sea. She instinctively paused at the spot where she remembered following Badriya, the neighbor's daughter, to her rendezvous with her boyfriend Ibrahim from the Eastern Province, who was a student at Orouba Secondary School. Badriya used to buy Nora the coconut candy she adored so she would not tell anyone about Badriya's illicit dates with Ibrahim.

She drove the car especially slowly past the house of Abu Hussien Almahlawi. The place made her remember her poor friend Masoumeh. Nora pondered her whereabouts; the last she heard was that Masoumeh never married because she loved a man who was not of her religion. Accordingly, her family rejected him outright, but she remained faithful to her love. How difficult and unfair it was to have someone else choose a life partner for you, only to find you felt no love for him!

She could never forget the day when she was about ten and went with Masoumeh to the Hussainiya, a congregation hall for Shi'i commemoration ceremonies. That long-ago morning, Masoumeh's brother Hussein had fallen and injured his head; there was blood everywhere. They had dreaded the reaction of his mother, Aunt Sakinah, but to their surprise Sakinah took her son's head in her lap, saying, "Praise be to Allah, this is Ali's sword on Ashura, the blessed day." Nora had looked around, trying to see the sword, wondering where it was—and who was Ali? Masoumeh then whispered in her ear, "Today is Ashura, the day Muhammad's grandson Hussein ibn Ali died. I'll take you with me to the Hussainiya. You're always asking to see the rituals performed there."

Nora quickly devised a plan. "Wait until my mother falls asleep and I'll come with you."

When she returned home she asked her mother, "Why don't we go to the Hussainiya, like our neighbors, Abu Al Hussein's family?"

The piercing gaze of her mother used to frighten her, for she had a strong personality, a blend of tenderness, pride, and power; everyone consulted her on important affairs. Even Nora's father used to observe silence before her. She took Nora in her lap.

"Nora, my love, I've told you to stop asking so many questions. Abu Al Hussein's family has different customs than ours. It's not acceptable for Sunnis to go to the Hussainiya."

"Mom, but why?" Nora asked. "Maryam Khatoon gave you a Bible when you gave birth to my sister Mira at Sarah Hosman Hospital."

"This is their religion and she wanted us to know about it, but we, as Muslims, may not read their book," her mother firmly replied.

She was afraid to tell her mother that she, as a youngster, used to go on Sundays to their house, and Maryam Khatoon would distribute candy to the children, saying it was a gift; Nora used to take it and throw it away.

"Mom, Rose and Firyal, in the religion class, leave the classroom and go to the schoolyard because they're not Muslims; they don't attend the class and don't take the test. I have seen their certificates, indicating that they are not Muslims," she returned.

"Yes, Nora, that's why we must not listen to them—because they're not Muslims," her mother patiently said.

"Mom, what does Ashura mean? Aunt Sakina says it's a blessed day," Nora continued persistently.

Her mother's patience was exhausted. "Quit asking questions, Nora! The sun is blazing outside—come on, go to sleep. At four, Hanifa will take you to Kuttab."

"Mom, school in the morning and Kuttab in the afternoon?" she cried, protesting. Kuttab was a primitive elementary school where children could learn Quran, reading and writing, in addition to other basic things they would need to know.

"You may memorize two chapters of the Quran, which will benefit you," her mother smiled.

"All right, but will you hold a Tomina, a celebration, for me if I recite the whole Quran?"

"Why don't you first finish Juz Amma?" The Juz Amma is the last section of the Quran, but the one most easily memorized by children.

"Mom, the teacher Mutawaa bint Al-Zahab said that she will hold a Tomina for Hamad bin Boseif on Thursday," Nora said enthusiastically. "I want to go with them around the neighborhood, collecting gifts for completing the recitation of the whole Quran."

"You go to sleep now. We shall see when Thursday comes—Allah is generous," said her mother, giving her hope.

Nora went back and forth to her mother's room, deliberately talking to her until she was sure she was asleep in order to sneak out of the house, stealthily, making no sound at all. Masoumeh was waiting for her at the back door of the house. Nora made a final check to confirm that her mother was asleep.

"Mom, when will my father bring me the deer and the rabbits he promised me?"

Her father had gone to Al Batinah of the Sultanate of Oman. Her mother did not answer, giving Nora confirmation that indeed she was snoring. She hurriedly went to the back door.

"Where are you going, Nora?" Their Pakistani maid, Hanifa, caught her and firmly grabbed her hand. "Your mother will scold me about this."

"Hanifa, just for a few minutes, I want to walk with Masoumeh, and then I'll come back so you and I can go to Kuttab. Don't tell my mother—here, these five riyals are for you."

"Come back real fast, Nora," Hanifa said, taking the five riyals and stuffing them in the folds of her clothing.

Masoumeh, who was waiting patiently, looked relieved when she saw Nora coming.

"Argh, Masoumeh, my mother from one side and Hanifa from the other," she sighed.

"Let's go quickly—the Hussainiya is just close by," Masoumeh said.

On their way, Masoumeh chided her for wearing a yellow dress since Ashura was a day of mourning, but Nora hadn't realized that she should have dressed for the occasion. They entered a big house where all the women were wearing black. One of the women was holding a microphone, reciting sad melancholic verses, and the rest of them were wailing and beating their faces and chests rhythmically, matching her tune. Nora was so terrified of the scene unfolding before her eyes that it made her cry along with them.

"Hey you, girl! Um Yazeed, why are you dressed up in yellow?" one of the women yelled at her.

She did not understand what the woman meant. Instead, she carried her shoes in her hand and ran with full speed towards her house, her heart beating fast, wondering about the meaning of Um Yazeed and who she might be. Luckily, she arrived home before her mother woke up; her grandmother was washing, in preparation for Asr prayer. Nora went straight to her with a question.

"Grandma, who is Um Yazeed?"

Her grandmother just laughed and shook her head. “I have never heard of her. Is she someone new in our neighborhood?”

Nora decided to ask her Kuttab teacher Mutawaa bint Al-Zahab instead. However, this might not be the best day to do it; Nora had not memorized Surat Al-Burooj, the passage she was assigned, and was a bit afraid of being beaten with Mutawaa’s staff. She reckoned that the best thing to do was to go the kitchen and wash the dishes. Everyone was seated in front of Mutawaa bint Al-Zahab, their Qurans ready and open.

“Have you memorized Surat Al-Alaq?” Mutawaa shouted at Hameed.

“Yes,” he said, and started reciting from memory.

Fear swept over Nora. Remembering her plan, she suddenly stood up.

“Mutawaa, you have a lot of unwashed pots and pans. Shall I wash them?” she said with innocence.

“Very strange—Nora wants to wash the dishes! This we must see!” Mutawaa laughed. “Let’s see how she does. Rawya, go and help Nora.”

Nora went with Rawya to the kitchen, amid the laughter of the girls.

“Phew! I barely escaped the memorizing session,” she said. “Rawya, darling, please do the washing and I pour the water for you. Otherwise, we both will get punished—you know I am not good at washing.”

"I know you, Nora—you're very smart. You cleverly managed to escape your turn in reciting Quran," Rawya said grudgingly.

Nora came out of her daydream and slammed on the brakes, a cry escaping her lips; she was inches away from hitting a man who was crossing the road. She sighed in relief. *Those Indians are suicidal—despite the presence of a jersey barrier, they still cross the road. It is impossible for them to abide by the traffic rules. There are pedestrian bridges and tunnels on Alwehda Street, but very few people use them. A nationwide media campaign should be launched to promote road safety awareness.* Unconsciously, her fingers turned on the radio. A song was playing, and her mind began wandering with the Egyptian singer Angham. The beautiful melody mixed with her own pain and memories.

By the time she finally arrived at the Shababeek Restaurant, the heat was intense and the sun was blazing. She had to choose a table inside the restaurant although the outside seating area was more appealing. She asked the waiter for a corner table so she could talk freely with her friend. Waiting for Salma, she passed the time grazing on most of the appetizers available on the menu and a mixed grill dish. She knew that Salma would be late as usual, as she was deeply in love with her work, never wasting a single minute.

"I'm on the way—don't forget to order the watercress and grape leaf salad for me," Salma messaged her.

Nora texted back, "Just hurry up! I have ordered all the appetizers."

She requested the waiter to bring three plates for three people. Time passed, slow and inevitable; it was approaching three o'clock, very late even for Salma. *That's not right,* Nora thought. *What might be the reason? I hope things are fine.* Nora called Salma's mobile several times, until she finally answered.

"Nora, darling, I'm very sorry. I was on my way to you, but they called me and said my father fell sick and they took him to the hospital," Salma said, her voice choked with tears. "This is where I am right now."

Nora asked the waiter to have the food wrapped up for takeaway so she could distribute it to workers and laborers along the way home. This had been her habit since the time she was with her Kuwaiti friend, Munifa, in Alexandria, where they used to pack up excess food and distribute it to the poor and needy.

She felt extremely distressed. She wanted to talk, to bare her soul, but with whom might she do that? She trusted no one but Salma.

Arriving home, Eisa was waiting for her. "Why are you late?"

"I got caught between a demanding job and congested traffic. You know how it is!"

"You always use that as an excuse!"

"What do you want me to do, buy a flying car?"

With that, Nora ascended the stairs to her room, knowing that arguing further with her husband would be a waste of valuable time and would never end.

Surfing through her mobile, she noticed a message:

"It's me, Muhanna, and you're my Nora—on my mind for more than a quarter of a century. Can I chat with you on WhatsApp?"

"What can I say after a quarter of a century? Give me back the heart that you pulled out of my body that day? How stupid of me, falling in love with someone whose real name I didn't even know. Now you come back to tell me your real name is Muhanna!" She texted her reply with trembling fingers, anger twisting the corners of her mouth.

"Say what you want to say. The truth is, my circumstances were neither convenient nor favorable then. We parted ways but our souls didn't, and I am sure you're still faithful to our love. I will explain everything to you. I have to go now, but I'll be in touch with you soon. Please save all of my numbers."

Nora was already texting a reply when he signed out, leaving her alone in her circle of suffering. She went through all the details in her memory, asking herself whether she was happy now that she had finally found her love, or sad that she might have to walk down that route of torment all over again. She found him and did not find him, both at the same time. His return brought back memories of her broken heart. *It seems that I have no right to love, but is love really bound by time or place or even age?*

A message from Salma snapped her out of her deepest thoughts: "Dear Nora, at seven, wait for me at the café at Lake Khaled." It was six o'clock; looking outside her window, she saw that Eisa's car was still outside. She swallowed, not sure how to tell him that she was going out. She was weary of his interrogations and questions every time she left the house. "Don't be late, where are you going, who are you meeting, stay home!"

In her mind, she wondered why he wanted her to stay home since he was not in the habit of doing so himself; he cared only for his business and wanted her to look after the house and the kids. This was his way of making her suffer, for he could not beat her, now that their kids were old enough to react.

The time now was six-thirty and he still did not leave, so she decided to call him on his mobile.

"Abu Khalid, I am going out to meet my friend. She's waiting for me—I'll be back soon."

"You go out every day—you don't know how to stay home at all."

She was used to hearing these words, which by now sounded like a broken record. She got out in a rush, heavy traffic facing her. She wanted to be there before Salma, so she took a short cut through side roads within the residential neighborhoods. Finally, she arrived; the first thing she did was order Osmanlia, a Turkish dessert that was Salma's favorite, along with Turkish coffee.

Salma came, waving at her, holding some books in her other hand.

"I know you're reserving this empty chair for that someone, but what's the matter, Nora? What's going on?" Salma sank into the chair opposite her.

"It's an affair of the heart, Salma, an affair of the heart."

"Are we back to the heart thing, Nora?" Salma said cunningly.

"Please, Salma, just listen to me. The vacant chair, Salma, you know, I want to talk to you about the vacant chair. Soon it won't be vacant any more, but I wish for no one to know. I trust only you with my secrets. You know something, Salma, I'm so happy!"

Her face glowed with life.

Unintentionally, Salma let out a cry of joy. "Finally! Congratulations, is this real? Is he coming? Should we order some juice for him? I want to see him and slap his face for the years of torment you've suffered. Tell me, how did you find him? But most importantly, after all this time, do you now know his real name? Where is he? Is he going to be late?"

"Calm down, please! He won't come here today. What's important to me is that I found him, or rather he was looking for me and found me. I need someone to talk with, and you're my closest friend. He told everyone around him our story, including his kids, saying that it happened to a friend of his. As a man, he dared not tell them that he was the star of our story, or should I say the oppressor."

"After all these years he came back looking for you—isn't this puzzling? Is it possible that his conscience got the best of him? Or maybe he didn't find anyone as honest and straightforward as you! All right, Nora, let it all out—unburden yourself and tell me. I am all ears and ready to hear the tiniest details. How did he find you? This is unbelievable! After so many years! Yet he could have found you a long time ago, since he knew everything about you. After all, you're the one he loved."

"Salma, what matters is that he finally did. Everywhere I go, I reserve a chair for him, and someday he may sit in it."

"Despite what he has done to you, you still stand up for him, Nora! What a pity, I must say. You want to go back in time, twenty-six years, and let love torment you again?"

"Let me live the dream at least once in my life, Salma. Let me feel happy for even a few moments, and let me talk to you about my feelings. You know that I have sacrificed my life, my youth, because of the backwardness of my family. They sentenced me to a soulless life, forcing me to marry my cousin, for whom I have never had any feelings of intimacy at all. Eisa put me through all kinds of torture. I tried to love him but he made that impossible—

his actions planted hatred deep inside of me. I have put up with him so he wouldn't deprive me of my children, whom I love more than life itself. All the while, though, my soul was traveling away with the person I loved. Fate kept him away from me for twenty-six years, making my faithfulness the longest recorded love story in the history of the whole world. You know, my romance should be in the Guinness Book of World Records!"

"All right, Nora, tell me the whole thing. How did he find you? I know that you knocked on doors, searching for him, and spread your pictures and news in all newspapers, using your contacts and influence. You even wrote about him."

"Yes, Salma, all my writings have been directed and dedicated to him. I knew he was a poet, and that's why I wrote and continued writing, even though I was suffering immeasurably. I kept on writing after losing track of him, hoping to find him again. Back in 1990, I faced the toughest moment in my life—I was at Athens International Airport, coming back home when I heard the news of the invasion of Kuwait. At that moment, I forgot all about the people I knew in my life, my friends and my family included, except for him. His image was standing vividly before my eyes, right there in the airport. I was so cold that my teeth were chattering, the cold of fear engulfing my entire body, stifling my words. I ran around like a mad person, trying to think of where to search for him, trying to find a telephone so I could call his number, which I had inscribed inside my heart, but it was to no avail. I tried to contact some of the people I knew, but the lines were down. The airport clock was pointing to ten a.m.; I called our home in Sharjah, only to find that they had not heard of the invasion. The sight of the people at the airport was terrifying—families crying, long queues at the telephone boxes, one man smoking his lungs into oblivion with clouds of smoke wreathing his head, a woman crying out in her Kuwaiti dialect, 'My home, my children,' an old woman fainting at my feet. And I was caught in the midst, shaking like a fish, kissing the forehead of the unconscious woman, my heart aflame with fear for the man I loved.

"A state of calamity prevailed over me; oh, how difficult those moments were. I agonize every time I remember them. My husband was shouting, 'Come quickly, we can board the plane now.' I heard the voice of a man crying, 'My parents, my country!'—that scene tormented me. It was then that I remembered the sensation of my love's tears falling on my hand as we sat in the café on the beach in Alexandria, one day before he disappeared. Cups of coffee filled our table. I still can smell the scent of his tears on my hand. Those same tears filled my life with pain. Ascending the stairs of the plane, I left my heart at the Athens airport with those Kuwaitis who were pondering their fate. The flight seemed longer than usual, since I was concerned for my love and his homeland. When we arrived at the airport in Dubai, we were met with sad faces and swollen eyes. Everyone was listening to the radio, waiting for news. What a misfortune had plagued our land!

"And all I could think of was him."

(4)

The mobile phone vibrated in her hand and its screen lit up, showing a new message. "Listen, Salma," Nora said with a sigh, "this is what he just wrote to me on Twitter: 'The most wonderful thing in life is love, but what's more wonderful is for loyalty to radiate with love.'"

"Well, I bear witness to your loyalty," Salma said.

"One moment, Salma, let me respond to this message on Twitter."

"Are you crazy? Don't tweet him yet—you might expose yourself. Nora, tell me the full story."

"It's now half past eight—Eisa will call me soon. You know how he is, right?"

Salma laughed. "I know him and I know that the one sitting before me is none other than Cinderella, who must return home before the clock strikes nine. I want to hear all the details, how he reached you, when, and where. Did you see him in Germany? You just came back from there recently."

"Wait, Salma, don't get carried away. I have not seen him—he found me through Twitter."

"What a pity! I can't believe you still haven't seen him, or even set a date with him!"

"Are you mad? How would I see him? Neither time, nor date, nor circumstances allowed us to meet, let alone the distance."

"I want to hear it all from you. I'm dying to hear all the details, so don't leave anything out."

"Believe me, I want to tell the whole world about this love," Nora said. "Sometimes I feel I'm going crazy, pinching myself just to check whether I'm dreaming or awake."

Her mobile phone's screen lit up once again. "Salma, listen to this—listen to what he wrote to me! 'How I have longed for you, to have you with me for life. But fate had the upper hand, it parted us, and all I could do was yearn and long in silence. I resorted to silence, longing for you.' And this is his second message: 'Come to me, you've stolen my moments of joy—nothing gives me pleasure without you near me. I wish words would help me express this insanity—my love for you—that has torn me apart and damaged my mind, for I can no longer be patient.' What do you think of this, Salma?"

Letting out a long sigh of excitement, Salma said, "What a sweet love story, Nora!"

Suddenly Nora felt a flash of anger. "I wish! What love story are you talking about, coming after a quarter of a century! This is nothing but madness of the soul." Nora stuffed her phone into her handbag. "I've got to go back, Salma. I don't want my husband to lecture me when I get home. Drink your coffee, it's getting cold. I'll take care of the bill."

Salma put her hand over Nora's. "You have time. You wanted to talk to me—let's talk. I will never forget the day I saw you searching amongst the Kuwaiti families that arrived in the UAE. You volunteered to work till midnight, helping them, while silently looking through the faces for a special someone, a face that was etched on your heart and soul, praying that no harm would come to him."

"It was the toughest year that any of us have ever experienced," Nora said with a pure tone of truth in her voice. "Yet, I feel I have suffered the most. My mind was paralyzed, looking through the newspapers and magazines for the names of the lost and the dead, banging my head with my hands, pining away and blaming myself for not knowing his real name. I phoned the hotel where we met in Alexandria, asking the receptionist for a list of the names of the students. The man refused, laughing at my strange request. I hung up the phone in despair. I went to Um Hamad's house under the pretext of asking about her daughter Amani, who was married to her Kuwaiti cousin. Abu Hamad was standing against his Land Cruiser that was laden with food and other goods for the Kuwaitis. I stood there, wishing he would take me with him, or at least help me in my search for my love.

"Do you remember the day of Kuwait's liberation? We were in Abu Dhabi at the time when we heard the news on the radio. We danced around, chanted, and cheered like crazy. I remember asking someone in the crowd, 'Do you work in the Ministry of the Interior?' Because I knew my love did. I wasn't sure what the man thought of me but he asked me back, 'Do you know someone there in particular?' I then decided to bail out on my question, since I didn't really know what to say. I didn't even know his name!"

"At first you thought he was the poet Hamoud," Salma reminded her.

Nora nodded. "One day, back in my university days, I was sitting in el-Haram Hotel with my Bahraini friend Munira, and I asked her, 'Have you seen the famous poet, Hamoud? He is with us in this hotel.' She answered, 'No, I haven't seen him around, I know him very well and I have attended some of his poetry evenings in Bahrain. By the way, Nora, who's the young gentleman who was sitting with you a while ago? Is he a new student?' Despite that answer, the thought that my love was impersonating Hamoud never crossed my mind."

"Love is blind," Salma commented.

"It must be. Several days passed, and he called me, letting me know that he had left the hotel and gone back to his brother's apartment. He sometimes behaved erratically, which worried me a bit, but I always managed to find excuses to believe him. That day, I sat in the hotel's café near the window and ordered Turkish coffee and gateau. Watching the sea, looking left and right, I really expected him to come back. The cool breeze kept refreshing my memory, reminding me of him.

"A lot of students were gathered in the lobby discussing and reviewing material for the upcoming exams. Some of them were preparing cheat sheets. One of them approached me; I recognized him since he was my classmate. He said, 'You always leave the exam hall early. I have cheat sheets and I can help you if you stay a little longer.' I nicely declined his offer, laughing. 'I don't want to pass by cheating,' I said. Although he was a handsome young man and girls' heads always turned to follow him with their eyes as he walked around, I never liked to be with him.

"Time passed, and my wait lasted long into the night. He never came, so I left the coffee and gateau and went up to my room, still waiting for his call.

"His call finally made it through, but with a troubling surprise. 'I'm in Cairo,' he said, 'and tomorrow I will depart to Kuwait. I will call you from there—you just wait for me every night at nine o'clock. I will be calling you,'

"I laid down the phone and cried my heart out. I sensed that it meant I would never see him again, and as it turned out, I was right. For a quarter of a century he has been away in person, but present with me in spirit."

"But why has he come back now?" Salma asked. "Tell me that!"

"I wish I knew," Nora said. "Oh, Salma, I wish you could come home with me in my car so we could continue our talk."

"But I have my own car outside! How about if we get together tomorrow and pick up where we left off?" Salma suggested, and Nora agreed.

They parted ways, leaving behind the beautiful Lake Khaled with its fine restaurants and musical fountain. The sight of the water canal, the walkways, the beautiful flowers, and the Eye of the Emirates had the power and charm to fill Nora once more with hope.

Along the way, in her car, listening to the Iraqi singer Kathem Al-Saher sing "Where Would We Run Away To," Muhanna's image vividly appeared before her on the windshield. Nora's face beamed with a bright smile as a memory swept her away to the second time they met, when he scolded her in the hotel for not wearing her abaya—the long cloak that was part of a modest woman's everyday dress. Being in a hurry, she had rushed down to the lobby from her room, wearing a hijab—a headscarf—but forgetting to put on her abaya. Suddenly the handsome man she'd met at the registration desk was at her side again.

"Where's your abaya?" he asked her in a low but firm voice. "You should never go out without it."

She nodded, her mother's words echoing in her heart: "Embraced with pride, the abaya gratifies the body." From that moment forward, she would always wear her abaya proudly.

Looking back, she realized that this would have been the perfect time to start a conversation—for instance, she could have asked about his college or university, since el-Haram hotel was the preferred residence for students from the Gulf. But she had given no thought to such mundane matters; her thoughts were drowned in love.

Suddenly, she pressed hard on the brakes; she would have slammed into a school bus if it had not been for God's grace. She glorified Allah for saving her and the many young lives on the bus. As she took deep calming breaths, a beautiful little girl waved at her through the bus window.

(5)

As Nora calmed herself from her near-accident, the school bus drove away. It took her back to her own childhood. She had always wanted to ride the school bus, but her father forbade it, forcing her to go to school with the family's driver instead. She used to cry and beg him to let her take the bus, since all of her friends were riding it, telling her interesting stories of the places they passed through. Her father's love had somewhat worn Nora out and his fear for her had her worried; he was so protective of her that whenever she went on a field trip with the school, he would insist on taking her there himself.

At an early age, she had recurrent tonsillitis, which sometimes left her feverish and sick. Eventually the doctor decided that it was best to go with a surgical solution. But her father, who was very fearful of the consequences of general anesthesia, refused to go through with it; he had heard that in the Iranian city of Shiraz, they regularly performed such operations with only local anesthesia. So he decided that the family should travel to Sharaz so Nora could have the surgery done there. At the time, Dubai TV was showing a series entitled "About My Room" starring Nora's favorite Lebanese actor and actress, Abdul Majid Majzoub and Hind Abe Elamea. Nora balked outright at the idea of traveling and cried real tears, pretending to be afraid of the operation. In truth, she just didn't want to miss a single episode of her show.

It was her second time to board a plane. They landed in Shiraz, the green city, with its charming gardens and giant trees that lined the road all the way from the airport to the hotel. One of the laborers, an Iranian from Qeshm Island who worked in Nora's father's plant, accompanied them on the trip, bringing his family along. The hospital was large and spread out, causing Nora to be afraid in earnest. Furthermore, in the operating theater, the sight of the medical equipment and the staff all dressed in green scared her a great deal.

In half an hour, the operation was over and Nora walked out of the operating room on foot. Suddenly she felt dizzy; and when she opened her eyes, she saw a tear running down her father's cheek, while her mother was screaming in panic. She smiled at her father to calm him down and let him know she was fine. The doctor had recommended that her food should strictly consist of varieties of ice cream and soup. In the evening, Nora's father and his employee brought her all kinds of ice cream and soup from downtown Shiraz, but the pain she was feeling precluded her from swallowing anything at all. All the while, Nora's father watched her with hurt-filled eyes.

Several days passed before she started recovering from the operation. In Shiraz, she went to the cinema for the first time in her life, although there were two movie theaters in Sharjah—the Sharjah Cinema and Al-Hamra Cinema. Nora could not recall the name of the hotel where they stayed, but the street's name was Moshir, one of the liveliest streets she'd ever seen, where some women were strolling around in short dresses and skirts, similar to those in Arabic movies. Conversely, some conservative women were wearing colored and decorated abayas, in stark contrast to the black abaya and burqa worn by Nora's mother and the women back home to veil their faces. Nora was thrilled to see her father wearing a suit for the first time, giving up his traditional garments; he looked like a real gentleman. The receptionist occasionally asked Nora, "Do you like Ali or Omar?" She would innocently answer him back, "My father is Omar and my brother is Ali." When she got older, she realized what he was after with his vicious question.

Almost all the affluent people of Sharjah used to spend their summers in Shiraz. The movie theater was right next to Nora's hotel; she went there along with her friends and cousins and sat in the front row. The first film she saw was a western; a man was riding a horse with a gun in his hand, looking as if he was coming towards her. The sound was so loud she screamed with fear, for it was her first experience with sound effects. Someone came to her, trying to calm her down, saying, "Don't be scared—he is inside the screen, and won't come out. Try to relax and enjoy the movie." After she survived that experience, the family got into the habit of going to the cinema every day, watching the same film over and over again.

Suddenly the mobile phone vibrated, startling Nora back to the present and announcing an incoming WhatsApp message. "Oh, such a wild moment to embrace a dream that hurts the heart, making it grieve!"

Choked with torment, Nora swallowed hard, reading the message again and again. Absorbed in thought, she accidently hit the car in front of her. She stopped the car, thanking God that it was only a minor collision.

The man in the other car rolled down the window; he seemed to be an Arab expatriate. "What should we do now?" he asked.

"I don't know," Nora said, momentarily baffled.

"Let's get out of the road and park our cars on the shoulder," the man advised.

They both parked their cars in the fiercely blazing sun. Nora was suddenly engulfed with a wild headache. She was looking for an escape even though her car was insured, which meant that the insurance company should handle all involved costs. Yet she knew the boring routine of the police and the bureaucratic procedures of the insurance company, in addition to the time it would take for the traffic police to answer the call and arrive at the scene. Valuable time would be lost, while she would be sweltering in the sun's natural sauna bath.

She asked, "How much do you want to repair your car? The damage is minor and your car is kind of old."

"A thousand dirhams," the man replied.

"But that is too much! It would be better to call the police and let the insurance company take care of it," she said with a touch of firmness that seemed to surprise the man.

"All right, just give me eight hundred dirhams."

She paid him the money and drove off in her brand new but slightly dented Range Rover, planning to tell no one about the incident, for if her husband knew, she would have to endure his yelling and scolding, and listen to his unnecessary lecture. *I can take care of my own car*, she thought, and called her brother, asking him to send his driver to take the car to the agency for repair before her husband got back from work. She would tell her husband that the car was in the shop for a regular periodic inspection.

Her daughter called. "Mom, I found a great designer in the Jumaira area. I liked his design. It costs eighty thousand dirhams, but he would buy it for half the price if I ever wanted to sell it."

"All right, Alia—if you like the design, then go ahead. This is your dream night; may Allah grant you happiness." She leaked a deep sigh, praying that her daughter's luck would be better than her own. She generally let her daughter choose whatever her heart desired. Nora befriended her daughter and son, believing it was a good way to raise them. She loved to join their parties and events, and help them select their clothes. She taught them the importance of self-confidence and clarity.

For her, things had been different. She had not been given much of a choice! She had lived her childhood joyfully as a pampered girl, enjoying frequent travels and fun. Having everything new in the market in her possession, she had stirred the envy and jealousy of everyone else around her. As a teenager, she was a crowned princess in her father's house. She had never had to set foot in the kitchen, for her father was afraid she would get hurt or burned.

But while she was still at college, her mother announced it was time for Nora to be married. She dissolved into tears; what else could she have done in the face of such unfair family rules, which deprived her of her right to say no? They chose a husband for her, and she could do nothing but agree to their order. That unjust arrangement destroyed her dreams, forcing her to surrender and accept their sentence without defending herself.

When her mother told her that her marriage was planned for the following week, she could think of no one but Aunt Samira, the Bahraini woman who used to tell her how she defied her family and country in the name of love, marrying a Pakistani man named Abdulhameed, and fleeing the country. With heavy steps, she trudged towards Aunt Samira's house, and at once the older woman took her in her arms.

"What's wrong with you, my most beautiful bride in the entire city?" Aunt Samira said.

"You should say the most unfortunate bride! I can't even find a shoulder to cry on! Tell me, Aunt Samira, how did you run away with your love? How can I marry someone for whom I have no love?" she said, her eyes welling up.

"Take it easy, Nora. You will grow to love him with time. Don't lose your family over this and lead a lonely life like me."

Nora shook her head stubbornly. "Why are we girls condemned to a destiny of arranged marriages within family, while the boys have complete freedom to choose their partners? I don't want to get married now. My dream is to finish college first. I have only completed one year. Should I run away to Egypt and continue my studies there? This thought is haunting me, Aunt Samira!" Sobbing like a child, she rested her head on Aunt Samira's chest.

"Nora, don't even think of such an insane idea! How would you live in Egypt, you crazy petted girl? Wouldn't college require tuition and expenses?" Aunt Samira caressed Nora's head. "I feel sad for you, Nora, and share your pain. I know you're in love with someone."

"How did you know?"

"I have been there before and I have writhed in the pain of love and involuntary alienation. As for your question about my marriage to Abdulhameed, you know our customs here in the Gulf—a girl must wed one of her relatives. But my problem was something far greater than yours. He was a foreigner, and not just any foreigner but a Pakistani! Since I was a little girl, my family committed me to my cousin, but I wasn't attracted to him—he was simply a relative to me. Abdulhameed, who was working with my father in the seaport, used to come to our house, and the spark of love ignited between us. Being forward and bold, I confessed to my father, but he slapped my face. I can still feel it to this day—it gives me the chills. He locked me in my room, and my mother used to spit her words at me like poison arrows. I starved myself until I got sick, and finally my father caved in and brought the marriage official to join Abdulhameed and me in matrimony. But he ordered me to leave the house with only the clothes I had on. I was dead in his eyes. My father still hasn't found it in his heart to forgive me. Nor has my mother, keeping her pain buried deep in her heart. Every now and then, I call our house, but as soon as I hear my mother's voice on the other end, my words freeze upon my lips. I hang up the phone, wordlessly. This is my situation now, Nora."

"How long have you been living in such estrangement?" Nora asked.

"Five long years have passed. To make it worse, Allah has granted me no children to keep me company!"

"Aunt Samira, tell me, how could I live with someone while my heart is with someone else? The sheer thinking of this love makes me scared. You know my mother, right?"

"Yes, dear. Aunt Amna's word is her bond—no one could stand up to her."

"Even my father has no say in things, for she is the head of the family. To this day, I'm still puzzled why she had agreed for me to study abroad in Egypt with my brother. It must have been one of the miracles of our age! Yet, I wish she hadn't," Nora said sadly.

"Is he an Egyptian, Nora?"

"No, Auntie. He is a Kuwaiti. He was an external student like me, staying at the same hotel as the other students from the Gulf states. Then he left during the final examinations." This was the first time she had confided in Aunt Samira. "I haven't heard anything from him since. He just disappeared."

"Right, and you didn't try—"

"I tried, but he never answered."

"Nora, my advice to you is to marry your cousin and continue your studies after you are married. Don't risk losing your family. Believe me, with time you'll be able to forget."

"The first time I saw him, it was like my heart leaped out of its place. I tried to get him out of my mind, but I couldn't."

"Calm down, dear, and just go home before they miss you. You know that Aunt Amna doesn't approve of you talking with me."

Dragging her heavy feet behind her, she wiped her tears. A voice deep inside urged her to run away, while at the same time, Aunt Samira's voice advised her against that. She screamed aloud, "Enough, enough."

The voice of her mother brought her back to reality. "Get ready. In the evening we will go to the dressmaker to take your measurements."

"Yes, mother," she said. She walked into her room and threw herself on the bed. Everything around her looked sad, even her books and letters. She turned on the radio, a request program playing the Egyptian Hani Shakir singing "Allow Me To Love." *Why this song at this particular time?* she wondered. It felt as if everyone around her were torturing her, leading her to the death chamber, killing her soul, but leaving her body intact.

Her eldest sister knocked on the door. "Come out and see. They have brought the invitation cards—they're looking great. We will distribute them, starting tomorrow. How many cards do you need for your friends?"

"I don't need any, Hessa. I'm just tired, and Mom wants me to go with her to the dressmaker," she replied, choking back tears.

Her sister embraced her. "What's troubling you, Nora? Why are you so sad?"

"I don't want to be married now!" she cried. "I want to finish my studies first. I want to return with Jamal to Alexandria where I already started my studies last year. Jamal will have the chance to attend his exams. I have passed my first year, and this is the second. Why does everyone want to deprive me from studying?"

"Nora, you know mother. She won't go back on her decision. Eisa is your cousin, and I think he wouldn't mind you finishing your studies. Come on, get ready, we will go to the dressmaker. Father has already ordered your wedding dress from Lebanon. It will be brought back here by his secretary, Ghadah."

A new message brought Nora back to the present, lighting her heart along with the screen of her mobile phone. It was he; it was as if he had become a teenager once again.

He wrote to her, "You, my first and last love—your face is the purest in this world—the finest my eyes have ever seen." She texted him back: "For as long as I shall live, this fantasy will remain—this pain will accompany me even if I fake a smile, for our eyes always reveal our sorrows."

How much I have loved you, Muhanna! You left me for so many years and today you came back to tell me I am your first and last love! The sheer thought of meeting you online was difficult—difficult—how much you wronged me when you did not tell me your real name. The only thing I had from you was the line you wrote in my notebook. I committed it to memory: "O God, gatherer of the hearts of lovers, unite those separated by the nights." The shoes you bought for me, I kept for many years until they got worn out. Remember the day when we got out of the hotel and took a taxi, and the accident that forced us to get out of it and take another? Yet a new accident took place, so finally we walked towards the beach and sat in a café, staring at the waves. Whenever I tried to take a picture of you, you would take the camera from my hand, and take a picture of me instead. Even a small token, as a picture of you, you would not let me have. You had me living in a gorgeous fantasy.

Alia walked in with a joyful air, snapping Nora out of her reverie. "Mom, the designer called. Please come with me—today is my first dress trial, and I want no one else but you to see me in my wedding gown. Our appointment is at six, Mom, but we must leave here at five. You know how traffic is."

"All right, Alia. Has your father come back from work yet?"

"Yes, and like usual, he had his lunch and went to his room. You know how he's addicted to news, wrecking his nerves following the latest crisis!"

"You're right, Alia. The whole world might change but your father wouldn't, since he saw virtue in the way things were. This has been our most challenging conflict."

She drifted with her thoughts to the time when her own wedding gown was brought from Lebanon; it was stunning, causing a stir among all her friends, becoming the center of their talks and attention. At first she refused to wear it, and when she finally did, she experienced neither pleasure nor happiness.

Ever since she was a child, she had dreamed of going to college in Egypt. But since her family did not approve of this, an alternative solution was found; she could be an external student, similar to being an online or correspondence student, at Beirut Arab University, which had a branch in Alexandria. She had taken her admission exam in Sharjah and passed with a high score. Once admitted to the university, she was able to study from home; she only needed to come to Alexandria for about a week to prepare for and take her exams. She certainly had not planned on meeting the man of her dreams in the short time she was there. Still, she had always known that her family made pursuing college studies conditional on her marrying a man of their choice, so she knew she had no right to object or even mutter her own opinion on the matter.

"I just want to study—to continue my education," she summoned the courage to tell her mother.

"After you get married, you may discuss the matter with your husband," her mother said.

Listening to the beat of the music around her, every sound was like nails being hammered into her head. All the while, his image was all she could see in her mind as the makeup lady was doing her face. Tears streaked the color on her cheeks like a rainbow.

"We only have a few minutes left," the Lebanese lady said, adding, "Please try to hold yourself together. I'm tired of wiping your tears and redoing your makeup. But why do such beautiful eyes have so much sadness? Why are you in tears? Should I call your mother?"

"No, please. I will stop, but don't tell my mother. How do you expect me to be happy while I am being slain?"

Her daughter's voice snapped her out of her thoughts. "Mom! Mom, you daydreamer, where have you been?"

"Alia, you naughty girl, I'll miss your playfulness. Where are you going to spend your honeymoon?"

"Switzerland, my most beautiful mom—and you're coming with us."

"My darling, my God grant you happiness, but I'm thinking of spending this summer in London. I haven't been to London since the eighties, after your uncle sold our family apartment in Queensway."

"Looks like Mom is yearning for England."

"I just wish your father would agree—I may travel with my sisters. I'll have enough time to decide after your wedding."

"You need to decide pretty soon. You know how expensive ticket prices get in the summer, and the Gulf Arab people will all be traveling to Europe as the situation gets worse in this part of the world. Syria has become a complete ruin, Egypt is suffering daily rioting everywhere, Iraq is on the verge of starvation with its displaced citizens, Lebanon is chafing under divisive sectarian problems, and we have almost forgotten about the Palestinian problem in the middle of this so-called Arab Spring. We got distracted from our main cause, for what is the aim behind all of this? So we would head towards Europe? How painful the situation has become in the Arab world!"

"They call it Arab Spring, but actually it has become Arab Fall and Destruction," Nora observed. "It's painful what we have become and the depths we have reached. Our biggest problem now is in Yemen. Our men answered the call of duty and went side by side with the Saudis to free Yemen from the hands of a repressive force. Every day we have new martyrs. Why have we become like this? Ah, Alia, you have opened the door of pain while I'm getting prepared for the wedding of the most precious person in my life!"

As the screen of her mobile phone illuminated, a faint smile swept her away. "Alia, this is your Aunt Salma. She's sent me a message. You can bring the car around while I text her back," she added, trying to hide her lie.

The letters flickered on the screen. "I am a kingdom, bordered by my memories of you, your passion is its sea, getting close to you is the bridge leading to it, your heart is its capital, and our love is its port."

She read the message over and over, then she wrote him back: "Whenever I got closer to a moment of joy, the days wipe it out, as if I'm being tracked by misery. This is how it is—love is like a mirage on my road and my lover is nothing but a myth."

She was jolted back to the moment by the sound of the horn of Alia's car, so she grabbed her purse and headed outside.

"Mom, I need to pick up my friend Abeer. She wants to see the dress too."

"All right, go on, Alia. Let me sit in the back and your friend can sit in the front seat with you. Take Alwehda Road, it's faster."

"No, Mom. Mohammed bin Zayed Road is faster," Alia said. "I don't want to go through Deira—the traffic signals there are unbearable. Here's Abeer, waiting by the door."

"Morning, Auntie Nora! Why are you sitting in the back?" Abeer asked.

"Abeer, darling, I want to be relieved of the troubles of the road. If I sat in the front, Alia's driving would terrify me."

Laughing, Abeer sat in the front seat, while Nora took her place in the back.

(6)

The WhatsApp blazed with his words. "Why do you still think it's a dream, Nora? One day it shall come true. I have shared our story with all of my friends, not to mention my sons and daughter. They all were sympathetic with it and my daughter was quick to say that the lovers should meet," he wrote.

Nora responded instantly. "You were bold enough to tell the story, earning their sympathy, but you didn't dare tell them that you were the real-life hero of this story, that you're the one who left me for all those long years, not caring to tell me your real name! All I had from you was a phone number. I don't deny that you've called me and sent me few messages in the past week or so, but for twenty-six years you just vanished without a trace. What could you say to justify that?"

"Nora, what could I have done differently?" he asked. "My uncultivated father threatened to divorce my mother if I didn't marry my cousin. Two years after my marriage, he gave me back my freedom of choice;

but by then you were already married, and I had lost you. Still, I kept looking for you. I was the one who found you after twenty-six years, right? You were always in my heart, and the minute I found your number I called you."

"I don't know—I really can't believe all of this. I hated all men because of you, and lost trust in people, including those very close to me. But before long, I would go back, overwhelmed by a nostalgic yearning, looking for justification to continue loving you, for you were the sweet dream that provided me with strength. In every lecture I gave, you stood by my side. You were always with me in all of my successes, the thought of you leading me to yet more success," she wrote him back, yearning softening her eyes.

"My love, please excuse me, I have something urgent to do, but I'll be in touch with you when I get a chance!" He sent his message and signed off.

"Mom, where did you drift off to, a topic for a new article?" Alia said teasingly, taking her eyes off the road for a second and looking at her. The buzzing of her phone saved her from Alia's naughtiness. It was her sister Khoula.

"Hello, Khoula, what's up? I wasn't expecting a call from you at this hour."

"Dear sister, I want to know the date of Alia's wedding so I can book a flight to London afterwards."

"Really, Khoula? How wonderful! Coincidentally, just today I was talking with Alia about traveling to London as I missed being there. Anyhow, please book a seat for me too. Will Abu Omar join you?"

"No, Nora, you know he works in the Ministry of the Interior. It would be difficult for him to ask for a leave. But Omar will accompany us along with our sister Huda."

"All right, I'll let Abu Khalid know. The wedding is on July 17th, and you can book our travel on the 25th of the month, okay?"

Laughing, Alia gently interrupted her, "Okay, Mom, it's good you decided on the travel date—you stilled my heart. Please enjoy your time with my aunts, especially with Aunt Khoula who adores London and knows its streets by heart."

When Nora was back with herself, she drifted into a daydream, recalling the time he talked to her about London and how he loved sitting in a café in Hyde Park, opposite Queensway. He told her of the exact location of the chair where he used to sit and think of her and their times together.

"I used to drink something other than coffee," he once told her. "I used to drink so I could forget my pain and sorrows."

The car swerved suddenly, careening her out of her memories. "Watch out, Alia! Why are you speeding? Don't you know that Jumaira roads are the prettiest in the country? This road here is not for speeding but for leisurely driving, so we can enjoy the scenery. Look over there, it's Burj Al Arab Hotel—see how tall and pretty it is. Let's enjoy sightseeing, Alia!"

Abeer agreed. "Aunt Nora is right, Alia. Why are you going so fast? Stop at the cafeteria over there—I want to have some Karak tea."

"I see that you're in agreement with your Aunt Nora, Abeer. The tea is on you, Abeer, and you might strike luck and be the next one to get married after me," Alia said with a hint of mischief in her voice.

Their laughter filled the air. Alia stopped at the cafeteria and ordered three cups of Karak tea, in response to the wishes of her mother and her friend.

****

Muhanna was sitting in his office, in his police uniform, surfing Google to see what Nora had written over the years. Suddenly he heard someone saying, "There's an accident at Salwa district near the Multipurpose Cooperative Association, involving a vehicle with a UAE registration plate." Hearing the country's name, he sprang up and rushed out like a mad person, for it was the country of his love.

He asked the policeman, "Where exactly did the accident happen, Ahmad? Did any of the passengers get hurt?"

"No, sir. I'll attend to the accident and find out what and who caused it."

"I'll go with you because they are our guests," he said.

"No need to bother yourself, sir. It's a minor accident. I'll take care of it."

The policeman was wondering why he was asked to be there himself. *What's going on? I must take care of it well*, he thought.

Back in his office, Muhanna began thinking to himself. *Can you hear me, Nora—can you sense the eagerness and yearning of my soul? I see your image in my cup of tea, I hear your sweet voice with every note of soft music, I see your face in the windshield when I drive home from work. You are with me every second of the day. You see, Nora, you thought wrongly of me; I admit that I was selfish and that I committed a serious mistake in not telling you my real name, and I even confess that I didn't allow you to take a picture of me. But believe me, I went over the top looking for you. You couldn't imagine the number of times I went back to Alexandria, visiting the places where we had been together. I used to visit my friend Mustafa and bare my soul to him, talking about you. I had him try to help me think of the best way to find you. You know, the day I left you and went to Cairo, it was because my father had called me, asking me to return and marry my cousin. How could I ever tell you that?*

I made a scene at the Cairo airport, and they were about to put me in jail, Nora. I bribed the archive staff at the university to find me your address or any clue that would lead me to you, for you changed your phone number when you married. Yet the word "Sharjah" was all that I knew about you. I have visited Sharjah several times, wandering its streets, hoping to get a glimpse of you. I was afraid to seek help from any official organization, because I didn't want to cause trouble for you. Ah, Nora, you could never imagine how much I have loved you. As seeing you was not possible, you remained alive inside my heart and my soul. Love does not kill the lovers. Rather, it keeps them hanging by a thread between life and death.

The ringing of the phone snapped him out of his thoughts. "Sir, the accident was minor. As per your orders, I have dealt with the guest with sincere politeness," the policeman said.

"Wonderful, Ahmad. This is exactly what I expect from you," Muhanna said.

He expected a lot from himself as well. He devoted all of his time to his work. Entirely forgetting himself, he would sometimes go to work at six in the morning and return home at four in the afternoon, or even beyond. At home, he would sit with his children, helping to raise them and solve their problems, acting as both father and mother, filling the void created by their mother who had ditched her responsibilities and abandoned them. In his spare moments, he resorted to searching for his lost love, aiming to find his true heart, the one who loved him more than anyone else.

He grabbed his phone, looking for Nora in Twitter; she had gone silent for few days because he sent her a WhatsApp message that said, "Yesterday, my wife returned home. I didn't want her to stay, but I couldn't refuse my mother's plea and my kids' wish. Please forgive me, sweetheart."

He came upon what she had written on Twitter, which had become sort of an outlet for her: "I gave you all my faithfulness, and this is how you think of me, a station on your way!"

He texted her back, "Don't kill me, don't hurt me, stop destroying me with your words, for they feel like daggers driven into my heart. You killed me as a young man—don't tear me apart now that I have aged in your love, and have nothing of value but you. I have placed the torn pieces of my heart at your feet."

She was quick with her reply message: "I too have been searching for my heart, only to find that it has fallen into a well, trying to breathe the whispers of passion, feeling abandoned by the one who ripped it from my body and continued on his way, not looking back once."

****

After sending that last message, Nora couldn't bear it anymore, feeling a pressure and tightness in her chest, wanting to cry out and not being able to utter a sound. So she turned off her mobile phone, closed the door of her room, and buried her head, like an ostrich, under the pillow, falling into deep sobs. This is what she had done many years before when her husband beat her. She was careful then not to allow her kids to perceive her weakness. She made sure she looked strong in front of them, in front of her family, and everyone who worked with her. She always stood tall and confident while delivering her lectures, but within the confines of her room—her private kingdom—she used to cry and cry. She was clever in hiding the bruises on her body from the inquisitive eyes of the world.

But there she was again, crying, but not knowing why! Was it a feeling of jealousy, or a fear of a new caprice from the same man who left her after stealing her heart? She bedewed her pillow with tears.

Abu Khalid called upstairs, "Where are you, Um Khalid? Come and hear the news. There was a terrorist bombing attack at a mosque in the Alanoud district in Dammam. A brave young man foiled the suicide attack by sacrificing his own life, saving the lives of scores of worshippers." He added with a touch of sarcasm, "They say his mother is a famous writer—I'm sure you know her, since you know all the writers, and many of them are your friends."

She got up from her bed, shocked by the news that rocked her to the core. Standing in front of the mirror, she wiped what remained of her tears from her face, then walked out saying, "There is no power or strength save in Allah. Even worshippers have not been spared from the dangers of terrorism. Why do they betray their own motherland—why target the innocents who are simply their brothers and sisters? The famous

Palestinian poet Ghassan Kanafani was very right when he wrote:

> 'Away with those who sold their integrity and direction
> Racing, slyly, to violate the mosques,
> Targeting the bowers and prostrators.'

"This great poem fits our current time—it reflects what's happening to us and around us today. These traitors really forgot the Palestinian cause and busied themselves with fueling conflicts in their own motherland. You should go back and use your minds—don't let the enemy control you. How could you kill your own people! God, bring us together."

Alia walked in, troubled by the news. "Mom, you must have heard about the terrible attack on the mosque in Dammam. It's even worse that this happened on a Friday, the day when family members should be together. Can you imagine the grief and sadness that cloud the hearts of mothers, wives, fathers, and sons, those who lost their dear ones on this day? Do you know the writer Kawthar Al Arbash? It was her son who fell victim to the murderous attack. There she is now, talking about him—come and listen to the mother of the martyr Mohammad."

"My son is gone," said Kawthar on TV. "He is a free man now. Mohammad chased the attacker away, protected the worshipers, and died. He left his children to be embraced every day by his friends and left my open arms yearning to embrace him. He said, 'One day the blind will see my fingerprint and the deaf will hear my line of conduct'—how true these words have proven to be. I would like to express my condolences to the mother of the suicide bomber. Your son targeted the best and the purest to kill—he couldn't have been more accurate in his selection. I know that your heart is grieving, just like mine."

Nora's eyes teared up. "I admire you, Kawthar. You're really a mother and a fighter, deserving all of our respect and appreciation. My Allah have mercy on your son Mohammad, and accept him among the martyrs."

As Alia walked over to turn off the TV, she saw the tears coursing down her mother's cheeks; an overwhelming sadness and stillness filled the room. So she rushed towards her mother to lighten the atmosphere. "Dear mother, you didn't tell me what you thought of my dress. You have been busy nattering away to your friend Salma. Didn't you like my dress, my most precious mother?"

"It's the prettiest dress for the prettiest bride I have ever set my eyes on," Nora said, wiping her tears with her palms and managing a smile. "May Allah grant you happiness."

"You're the prettiest, mom. Everyone says I look like you, so I know I'm pretty. I'm afraid all eyes will be on you during the reception."

"Alia, my beautiful, naughty girl, have you reserved the hall? How about the rest of the wedding party requirements? Do you need any help, sweetheart?"

"Of course I need you, dear mother, and I'm going to consult you. But Abeer is helping me with the selection."

The doorbell interrupted the conversation, and Salma walked in.

"Salma, my dear, what a great surprise!" Nora said, greeting her friend. "This is the first time you've shown up without prior notice. And as it happens, I'm in dire need of you. Come, let's sit in the bookroom. I have bought some new novels for young writers."

"Since the emergence of these new for-profit publishing houses, Nora, you can find new novels getting published every day," Salma pointed out. "I just hope that these books are up to par. Unfortunately, some books have remarkable titles and disappointing content."

"I remember that a few years back while in Cairo with my family, I was in a bookstore when a title of one of the books grabbed my attention— 'The Princess that Rocked the Throne of the Gulf.' The title was so intriguing, I bought the book. I couldn't wait to get home to read it. Regrettably, Salma, it was insignificant—definitely not up to my expectations!"

"I think the book rocked the throne of papers!" Salma chuckled. "A few days back, I finished reading a novel that won a grand prize. Unfortunately, it was not deserving of that prize, or any prize—but let's talk about something else."

Salma sat down in a comfortable chair as Nora shut the door. She lowered her voice a bit. "Tell me about the new developments with your returning lover. Reading your tweets, Nora, I understand their underlying meanings and the targeted person, since I know your story."

"You won't believe this, but someone wrote to me privately, saying, 'I feel as if all of your writings are for me.' I don't know what to make of this. Is he crazy? I've never seen him in my whole life."

Salma nodded. "One of my writer friends told me that whenever she wrote an article about social problems, she would receive several messages from people offering to help, confusing her for the troubled person in the article! Tell me, have you decided on your travel destination after Alia's wedding?"

"Yes. I will travel with my sisters to London."

"I'm sure you picked London so you could see the places where he used to sit, as he had told you. Have you agreed to meet there? It would be great if you did, Nora."

"My sisters and I agreed on the travel plan. I'm not really sure if his circumstances would allow him to be there, although he said he would like to try. As for planning a meeting, I'm a bit wary and hesitant, and he does not want it either. So we're leaving the matter to chance. It would be better for us now to meet in our dreams."

Her mobile phone suddenly rang in the living room, and she was forced to excuse herself from Salma so she could answer the caller. "It's my sister Khoula," she shouted.

"Hi, Khoula. How are you, Um Omar—what's up?" she said in a more normal tone.

"I want to let you know that I have booked the tickets," Khoula said. "My friend Um Obied will come with us, which suits me well—I like her company."

"It's all right with me—she's most welcome. My friend Salma is with me now, and says hello. Please don't forget to book a hotel in Queensway— you know that I want neither Edgware Road nor the Regent Park area. Also, I need a separate room for myself. As our sister Huda likes to say, I have my books and stuff. Let Huda be with Um Obied in a room and you with Omar in another."

"All right, Um Khalid. As you wish. I am aware of your frequent visits to Al-Saqi bookshop at Queensway, making you a distinguished patron. I also know about your addiction to the ice cream from the shop next to the Hilton," Khoula teased her.

"And what about you and your infinite love for Shepherd's Bush Market and its falafel wraps! Thanks a lot, Khoula. I know we'll have so much fun in London."

Would London just be a welcome respite with her sisters? Or would it be something more?

(7)

As Nora hung up the phone, Salma announced she'd have to leave; she needed to accompany her father to the doctor, since she had just received a call from her sister telling her that he had fallen ill again. Once more, Nora found herself alone. She walked into her room, casting a look at the calendar hanging on the wall opposite her bed, thinking of all the pain history had inflicted upon her and all the memories enclosed within its folds. He had told her, "Don't think of our reunion—leave that to time to take care of. Be assured that sooner or later, one day we will meet. I'm certain of that, and when we do we will never be apart again." She shook her head. *Is this man insane? Does he want to drive me crazy? He is so cryptic and vague—sometimes I believe him and other times I can't imagine what he's thinking.*

The previous week, she had a verbal dispute with her husband, and as a result he ignored her for a whole day. She vented her feelings in a tweet. "Pain overtakes you when you're certain that you're only a resting station in someone's life, and you must listen, empathize, and endure, while denied a voice of your own," she wrote.

But Muhanna thought that the tweet was about him and considered it an insult; his response was bitter, and it took Nora some time to convince him otherwise.

His presence in her life tormented her more than his absence. She was fearful that he would vanish from her life forever; she begged him not to leave her again. Yet she was almost certain that he would do it the minute he got occupied with something else.

She recognized that worry and sorrow followed her at all times; she whispered to herself, in a sad voice, "I don't know why he does this to me—is it because he's sure of my love for him? He's the one and only man who stole my heart, but why does he have so much ego? He has become like that Bollywood actor, Shahrukh Khan, who repeats one line in almost all of his movies, 'I'm certain you love me.' Why should the girl always be the one who loves, maintains loyalty, and sacrifices for her love, while the man simply stands by, tall and arrogant, to demean her?"

A message reached her on WhatsApp: "I love you, you're my love, you are the symbol of loyalty itself." She did not respond, unsure whether she even had the right to respond. But why should she torment herself? She thought of deleting the WhatsApp account and all her other electronic social media programs, trying to convince herself that Muhanna was not real, but rather an illusion that she should wipe from her mind.

Without the specter of Muhanna, she could continue to live her life, and celebrate the wedding of her daughter and the graduation of her son Khalid. She should not concern herself with him or even think about him. This was making her exhausted and unwell; what would come after this revived love had vanished again? Such questions tortured her, since she found no satisfying answers for his sudden reappearance in her life. Was his aim to torment her just because he was a man?

Again, she found herself whispering, "Oh my God, I'm about to go insane. I need someone to tell me that I'm in a dream—that it's all the work of my deceitful imagination. I want to wake up, I want to change my heart or mend it, I want to search for spare parts in the hearts market, for how else could I root him out of my heart? But are there, out there, similar hearts to mine? He has deformed it, making me suffer every day, forcing me to drink from his bitter cup of parting."

She threw her mobile phone at the wall, hoping it would break into bits and pieces. Unfortunately, it didn't break, and his messages continued to flow. She snatched the calendar off the wall and almost tore it apart, but stopped short of doing so—all her appointments were there. Her tears coursed unhindered as she picked up the phone and read his last message: "Your critical words on Twitter are fatal to me. I'm nothing but the wreckage of the years we've been apart. I'd put up with anything but you being angry with me—I can bear anything but that."

She took a deep breath, the volcano of pain subsiding in her chest. She read the message many times over before deciding to tweet him back: "I picked up a white daisy, smelled its velvety petals, but never played the flower game 'he loves me, he loves me not.' You were my first love, and you'll always be in my heart no matter if we're together or parted by difficult circumstances."

He wrote back: "This is how I know you, my love—you have a pure heart, not stained with hypocrisy or personal interests. This is what true love is. Good night, my love."

Turning her mobile phone off, she lay down, searching for the sleep that had deserted her. She had long wished for drowsiness to steal over her eyes without the aid of sleeping pills, but it was only a wish that never came true. Moreover, even the sleeping pills had stopped working. She had thought of every possible path that would lead her to find the love of her life. And she thought of the obstacles that blocked every one.

She remembered her friend Maryam, who lived a life of hell with her husband. Much like Nora, at a very young age Maryam married a relative who was bad-tempered. He never reasoned or compromised with her; his sole means of communication was yelling and beating. In middle age, she fell in love with another man, and as a result she demanded her freedom and asked for a divorce. One week after their separation, he married another woman, while she had to wait for her family to accept her idea of marrying a foreigner from another Arab country. She suffered a lot, but in the end she claimed victory and married the one she loved. Before her divorce, her son and daughter stood beside her until she gained freedom from the oppression of their father, but once she got married they abandoned her.

She thought to herself, *I would never go through the same experience that Maryam did. My children are everything in my life—I have sacrificed for them, raised them up right, and brought out the best in them until I saw them succeed in their lives. I couldn't endanger that bond.*

Nora eventually succumbed to the grasp of sleep. When she woke up, the morning sun had already crept into her room through the sides of the curtains. Hearing a knock on the door, she got up, laziness slowing her body, unruly locks of auburn hair covering the sides of her face. She tossed her hair behind her back and fixed her clothes before opening the door; it was her son Khalid.

"I got worried about you, my dear precious mother," he said. "It's already eleven o'clock. Sleeping this late is not a habit of yours."

"Khalid, my sweetheart, I stayed up pretty late last night, reading a new novel. Then I couldn't sleep until after morning prayer."

"Sorry to disturb you, my precious, I just got worried. I also need you to help my friend Khalaf, who wants to pursue a master's degree, but he was told that there were no vacant seats. I know that you are highly regarded and your word carries a lot of weight. I'm very proud of you, my most precious mother," said Khalid, using the power of warm persuasion in his voice.

"Fine, Khalid, I'll try. God willing, it will be all right. Write me his full name and the name of the college."

He softly kissed her on the forehead and left the room. She grabbed her mobile phone; there were numerous messages in her WhatsApp groups and Twitter. A message from Salma caught her attention: "A morning of roses to you, pretty one. Allow me to present you with the poem, 'Is It Tomorrow I Shall Meet You?', written by the Sudanese poet Elhadi Adam and sung by the diva Um Kulthum.

'Is it tomorrow I shall meet you? How terrified my heart is by tomorrow!
Behold my longing and burning, waiting on our date.
Ah, how much I fear this tomorrow of mine; still, I beseech it to come sooner.
I used to wish it to come, but I feared it as it drew near.
Yet the joy of getting closer to it came into sight.
It's how I live my life, a blend of bliss and suffering.
A soul burning like embers and a heart melting by the touch of yearning.
Is it tomorrow I shall meet you?

> You, the Eden of my love, my longing, and my insanity.
> You, the polestar of my soul, my freedom, and my chagrin.
> Is it tomorrow that your light will brighten the night of my eyes?
> Ah, the joy of my dreams, and the fear of my misgivings!'"

She nodded, wordless for but a moment, as if savoring the taste of the words, then wrote her response. "Oh, how beautiful are these words—it's as if they were written solely for me, except that I'm not expecting a date with him! I just wish to have as little as a grain of hope to see him, Salma. He neither gave me hope for a date nor an encouragement. We only meet in cyberspace, an arrangement that, I fear, may not last."

What else could she do to overcome the heavy dullness that dragged her down? The doctor had advised her to reduce her dependence on sleep medications, but her body had already been accustomed to them. Navigating toward the bathroom, she stepped into the shower; the cold water sluicing down her body helped her regain her balance, taking her into another world. She wished she could stay there under the water, dreaming of her childhood, the times when she used to go swimming in the sea with her friend, without telling her family. The waves, then, would flow around her legs, carrying her dreams, while her eyes fixed on the far horizon, watching the setting sun bid farewell to the sea and the sky.

The bathtub overflowed while she was lost in her daydream, playing in the water like a child. When she realized what had happened, she laughed at her childish behavior, for she had spent more than an hour in the shower. But all was not in vain—her memories and feelings turned into words; and she rushed back to her room, grabbed a paper and a pen, and started weaving the words into a poem about water.

Water

I searched for water in the heart of water
I heard him say: No water in the water
The mirage can never refresh or satisfy the thirsty
Whenever I got closer to the water, my breath dies
Indeed, the land yearns for the showers of rain
Like the leaves of trees, watching the last breaths of dew

****

It is the madness of a woman in the presence of darkness
The whispers that borrow their voices from the rays of the sun
I loved the pain and the suffering
Exuding pride that embraced my pillow

I have learned to dwarf pain in the presence of joy
Yet, my hurt equals my love of my city, with green feathers
For brooks, meadows, and lovely faces annul the pain
So said a maxim I have known since an early age

****

I painted rainbow colors on the canvas of the evening
This evening was the dream I long awaited
How long would my wait last before I finished my painting?
The frame refuses to embrace my picture
Fearing a long imprisonment that it wouldn't endure
The guard watches with drowsy eyes
As the colors edge closer to the frame's border
A dream that haunts me every night
I rise up, overcome again by the same dream
Would I be spending a lifetime, painting my dream?
Like water, flowing from springs, leaving only emptiness behind
The water, the dream, the emptiness, the image, the frame

This was her first attempt at writing poetry. She had phrased some of her thoughts and feelings before, but this was the first time she felt that she wrote something different. At once, she sent the poem to Salma, who was a distinguished, published poet, and then phoned her.

"What do you think of this poem I just wrote, Salma? I was in the shower, playing with water, and the words flowed naturally, so I quickly wrote them down before I forgot them."

"It's great, Nora. Love makes miracles. Please publish it, for it's really beautiful."

"No, Salma. You know me, I just write my thoughts and keep them to myself. I am only a writer, not a poet."

"Quite the contrary! You're a poet, and this great poem holds a wealth of meanings within its folds. You could even send it to your lover."

"This lover you're talking about hasn't been around since yesterday. He's often absent, and doesn't seem to care about me."

"You're possessive. You know he has work and family obligations and responsibilities, and can't simply afford to drop everything on short notice just to hang out with you."

"I do appreciate that, Salma, but he dedicated long years to his work and family while I was not part of his world. He should compensate me for all the years he has been away from me. Or else why did he show up again in my life? To torture me and kill me once more? As if once was not enough for him! He stripped me of my heart. He was a clever hunter and I was the naïve prey!"

"Yet eventually he came back for you. If he didn't love you, he wouldn't have searched for you, Nora. Besides, he told you about his past situation and circumstances."

"I don't know why I feel happy and miserable at the same time," she sighed. "My pain has worsened, and I'm now more worried about him."

"Never mind. What's important is that you make sure he is okay, and you wish him nothing but happiness," said Salma.

"I sacrifice my desires, my time, my happiness, and my own needs to make everyone else happy, but no one thinks of my happiness; it's as if I have no right to be happy. I'm merely the source of other people's happiness. Look at Abu Khalid. He never accompanies me to the hospital, even when I'm sick. I wish he would once take me out on a date to a restaurant, like other married people do. I've settled for going to restaurants in the company of my children."

"Well, at least you have them to comfort you," Salma said.

Nora waved her hand dismissively. "I'm sorry to have taken up your time, Salma. I must go now and get ready for lunch; you know Abu Khaled—I must be at the table even if I have no desire to eat. I'll seize the opportunity and tell him about my travel with my sisters to London. I'm almost sure he will lecture me, ruining my mood with his words. But what can I do? He doesn't like to travel, using his work as an excuse, but neither does he like me to travel even in the company of my family. I may actually have to convince him to let me go to London."

"May Allah help you—I know your husband," Salma said. "He is definitely a hard-hearted man, but I would think by now you must have grown accustomed to him."

"Yes, you would think so, wouldn't you?" Nora asked.

(8)

She walked out of her room, slowly descending the stairs; Abu Khalid awaited her, and she was thinking of how to start a conversation with someone who did not know how to converse.

She heard Eisa call her with his usual mocking voice. "Where are you, Nora? Come and sit with me—I want to have lunch."

"I'm here, Abu Khalid. I just don't feel like eating. I'm not hungry," she said.

"Come and sit with me, even if you're not hungry. So, what's new? Tell me."

"Nothing really, Abu Khalid. I'm still preparing for Alia's wedding, which is coming up fast. By the way, will you be taking your annual vacation so we can travel abroad after the wedding? As you know, the house will be boring once Alia leaves."

"No, I have not asked for my annual leave. Forget about traveling."

His response was no surprise to her. "All right, Abu Khalid. I may travel with my sisters, however."

"I see that you have already made your plans without telling me!"

"Yes, I'm going to travel with my sisters. I know you don't want to travel, so what am I to do here all alone? The times you're home, you keep to your room, and without Alia around to keep me company, I would be forced to run a dialogue with the walls of my room! Loneliness is a silent killer, but you don't feel it, do you?"

With her last words, she rose up and left the table, avoiding his hurtful and piercing words. She made sure he heard all she wanted to say. Wasn't he the one who never once bothered to help her with travel expenses? Why should she seek his permission? He had no claim on her. They were married only on paper, but she dared not let anyone on her secret. Instead she always painted him as a perfect man in front of people, while, in her eyes, he was quite the opposite.

Now in her room with a cup of coffee in her hand, she was sipping on it quietly to calm her headache and fix her mood, for Alia was about to show up and take her to the hotel to help her with the wedding stage decoration and arrangements, and Nora did not want to appear sad. She knew that Alia had already finalized most arrangements with her friend Abeer, but she still needed to oversee them from a distance and provide them with some guidance.

(9)

She was overjoyed to see Alia's name on the wedding invitation. All of the invitations she had received from friends and family never mentioned the bride's name; most families just referred to the bride as the daughter of someone. Nora had always wondered why this was so, since highlighting a girl's name was neither disgraceful nor sinful in Islam. Prophet Mohammad, peace and blessings of Allah be upon him, mentioned the name of his daughter Fatima and his wife Aisha on several occasions.

But things were changing. A new promising trend had begun to appear in which not only the bride's name would be mentioned on the cards, but also the mother's name as well.

In the hotel, she and Alia completed all of the party arrangements, and that made her happy since she wanted her daughter's wedding, a week later, to be the talk of the town. She returned home while Alia went out with her husband-to-be to shop for their upcoming trip. In her room, she started going through her WhatsApp and Twitter messages, which, to her disappointment, were all from friends, and none from Muhanna.

So many questions remained unanswered in her mind! Why did he suddenly appear in her life? What did he want and why was he treating her like that?

In his last tweet, he told her, "You resided first in my eyes, then in my heart."

In turn, she wrote, "I'm at my wits' end on how to respond to that. Should I have you in my eyes or in my heart?"

She hadn't heard from him since yesterday; at the same time, she had promised herself not to message him again, agreeing to endure pain and torment but not humiliation–she had had enough of that! She lay down on her bed, counting deer instead of sheep while waiting for sleep to come. For the first time in a long time, she fell asleep without taking any pills. When she woke up at eight a.m., the first thing she did was go through the hundreds of messages in her mobile phone. Yet again there were none from him; he had vanished from her world.

Donning her abaya, she jumped into her car and raced toward Sharjah International Airport. There, she asked the woman at the ticket counter about the nearest flight to Kuwait, and to her delight, there was one departing in less than an hour. She purchased a roundtrip ticket, intending to return that night. She ran to the designated gate, and within minutes, she was seated at the front of the plane. Most of the passengers were Asian. An hour and a half later, she found herself at Kuwait International Airport, not knowing what to do or where to go. It was Monday, so everyone was at work now, including him. She stood in the airport, thoughts crowding in her head. *Should I call him and tell him that I am in Kuwait to see him? No, he has always rejected the idea of going on a date. Should I surprise him with a visit to his office? Definitely not! It would be improper of me to do so, especially since I am both a wife and a mother. A woman like me, raised on the principles of Islam, deeply imbued with the values of right, goodness and virtue, should not get carried away with her emotions, come what may.*

But then what am I doing here?

In the taxi, she remembered that she had stayed at the beautiful Jumeirah Messilah Beach Hotel before, but it would be difficult to get there since she only had three hours before she had to go back to the airport. Instead, she asked the driver to take her to the Rumaithiya residential district, where her lover lived. As the driver circled the neighborhood, she looked in the windows, hoping, by a stroke of fate, to see him. Then, she asked the driver to take her to the Hawalli area, where Muhanna had told her he worked. She stepped out of the car after she asked the driver to wait for her, and approached the Ministry of the Interior building. Turning her head left and right, she felt her heart beating fast; she was a few steps away from the traffic department where his office was, thinking how easily she could get in there and ask to meet him as one of the customers. The voices of the customers reached her ears, and she easily picked his voice out of the crowd. Trembling, beads of sweat dripping from her forehead, she quickly retraced her steps to the car.

"Take me to the Avenues Mall," she told the driver, hoping her lover would intuitively sense her presence and come to see her. She bought some perfume at the Chanel store and spent the rest of her time sitting in a café, sipping mocha coffee. Two hours passed fast, yet he did not show up. She had to return to the airport and go back home before someone took notice of her absence.

Back in Sharjah, she returned to her car, dragging her feet in disappointment. Nonetheless, it had felt wonderful to set her feet on the land of her lover even though she was not able to see him.

She drove her car back home; and once in her room, she wrote him a message on Twitter since he told her he'd closed his WhatsApp account. "I just returned from Kuwait a while ago. I was there to see you, but couldn't tell you because I didn't want to cause any trouble or bother you. I drove around Rumaithiya and Hawalli. I was so close to you that I could hear your voice. I was about to go insane, but luckily I got ahold of myself. Oh, how I would have loved to have been one of the customers in your office, but my upbringing prevented me. I went to the Avenues Mall, then back to the airport. My return flight was at four p.m."

He wrote her back: "Why didn't you call me? How could you do that? You must be crazy."

In response, she wrote, "You didn't want us to meet. I don't know why, but I really missed you and I had to do something. Although I couldn't see you, it was comforting just to walk in the same areas where you lived and worked. It was a great adventure for me to fly alone for the first time—my friends have always bragged to me about how they booked roundtrip flights on the same day to go shopping, but I had never done anything like that before. I can't conceive how I did what I did, but I really did it! I might be insane but you're the reason behind my insanity, not letting me see you. You're selfish, and you'll always be. You don't care about my pain, my yearning, and my faithfulness to you all of these past years. All you care about is your work, your status, and your position."

Before turning off her mobile phone, she opened Twitter, and tweeted, "What if while you were asleep, in the middle of a long dream, someone came to wake you up, announcing that he was your dream. What if, caught in between wakefulness and dreaming, you found that he was nothing but pain and agony, and that you have become his prisoner until the time you wake up?"

She turned her phone off, not wanting to hear or read anything else; all she wanted was to concentrate on the wedding of her daughter. She wanted it to be a fabulous wedding that people would talk about and remember forever. So she called her friend Salma to come and help her address the wedding invitations, which she would send out with the help of her sisters. She needed to keep him off her mind and focus on completing the last-minute wedding preparations. He too must be busy with his wife who had returned to him; he only sent Nora a greeting message every now and then. She would greet him back, while burning inside, swallowing her pain, and praying to Allah to help her go back to her senses and not be a captive of her love.

Finally, the day of the wedding arrived. Wearing her navy blue dress, with silver beading and crystal detailing, Nora looked much like a princess. She was admiring herself in the mirror at home when Abu Khalid slipped up behind her.

"You know, you look great today. You and Alia look like sisters. Don't forget to recite the protection prayer," he said. It was the first time he had ever praised her like that.

The wedding party, held at one of the fanciest and most beautiful hotels of Dubai, was magical and spectacular, and featured an awesome ballet performance, a DJ, a live band, and soloists. All through the party, her friends praised her, highlighting her beauty and how she glowed as the queen of the party. Yet, he was still present in her thoughts, making her wish for things she could not have.

Taking a glance at her mobile phone, she noticed a message from him: "My heart and my soul are with you and around you wherever you go, sweetheart."

She texted her reply: "How I wish to break free from your chains and escape from your false love that has tortured me, since you are nowhere near me."

She felt fatigued, having wrapped up her role as the perfect hostess, standing, smiling, and greeting the invitees. So she booked herself a room in the same hotel so she could relax after the party, and then leave home the next morning to prepare for her trip to London the following week. She was lost in her thoughts about London, fantasizing that Muhanna would travel and meet her there. Khoula had already reserved an apartment in Queensway, near the Hilton Hotel, which overlooked Hyde Park, exactly as she had wanted.

But before she went to London, there was one more important event to attend. Her son's graduation ceremony was on Sunday; he made her very proud, graduating from the American University at the top of his class with a degree in Architectural Engineering. Brimming over with excitement, she was the first to arrive at the ceremony venue in the University City of Sharjah. She seated herself at the front row.

Khalid approached her. "My precious mother, this is my Kuwaiti friend, Adel. He wants to meet you. He's a big fan of yours, and he has read all of your published articles," he said, beaming with joy.

Her heart almost skipped a beat, hearing the mention of Kuwait. What if Adel might be Muhanna's son or the son of one of his friends, relatives, or neighbors? *Should I ask him if he knew him?* She struggled with the thought, but remembering the presence of her son next to her, she decided to save him from any possible embarrassment.

"Hello, dear Adel, I have heard a lot about you from Khalid. Allow me to congratulate you on your graduation. Please keep in touch when you return to Kuwait."

"Hi, Auntie! Khalid is my best friend, and I would never let anything break us apart. I have spent the best years of my life in Sharjah and so it will always be in my heart."

She sat down again to watch the graduation ceremony. When Khalid was called to the stage to be recognized as the top of his class, tears of joy poured down her cheeks and she knew that all of her hard work was not in vain. To her son and daughter, she was a mother, a mentor, a sister, and a friend. She had grown up with them, putting up with the unfair and sometimes brutal treatment of her husband. But today her children made her feel proud of what she had done.

Like the other Arabian Gulf states, the UAE and the local society in Sharjah were conservative, religious, and driven by tradition, especially when it came to women's rights. This had profoundly impacted Nora's behavior, compelling her to give up her rights, freedom, and joys of life, and to pretend to be content and happy despite the ill-favored circumstances and her husband's cruelty—for the sake of her children. But it had all come to fruition, as her son and daughter were embarking upon successful lives of their own.

She packed her bag with everything she needed for London, not forgetting her laptop computer and some novels. She was an avid reader of fiction and literary work, spending most of her time reading, and wondering if she would ever be united with her lover like the lucky heroines of the romance novels. She was all packed and ready for her flight to London in the morning. Khalid, who offered to take her to the airport, told her that she needed to be there at least three hours before the flight, so she planned to be on the road right after Fajr prayer, avoiding the morning traffic jam.

Khalid dropped her at the departure gate, kissing her warmly on the forehead. Her friend Um Obied, her sisters Huda and Khoula, and Khoula's son were awaiting her at the check-in counter.

Her toes tingled. Something wonderful was about to happen in London; she could just feel it.

(10)

"Good morning, Um Khalid! Congratulations on your son's graduation," her family chimed.

"Thank you. Allah bless you all," she said joyfully.

"Auntie Nora, where is Khalid? Why didn't he come into the airport with you?" Omar asked.

"I asked him not to, Omar. Today he has to get a physical for the national service. I feared he would be late for that, so I asked him to head directly to the service camp."

"I shall also join the national service right after I finish high school next year," he said.

"It opens the door to honor and glory for you, Omar. I wish everyone would join the service, for this is how we return the favor to our nation."

They carried out their check-in formalities and received their boarding passes. Then they headed towards the departure gate in Terminal 3, taking the metro. Nora dove into her handbag and pulled out an award-winning novel. Flipping through its first few pages, she realized that the novel was not what she had expected, certainly not to her taste. Yet, she insisted on reading it, taking it as a challenge to uncover the secret behind its implausible award.

The flight was about seven hours long, and surely Huda and Um Obied were going to make some smart comments about her habit of taking books with her everywhere she went. But in those last moments before the plane took off, Um Obied had her eyes tightly closed so she would not see the pre-flight safety briefing and demonstration. Instead, she was audibly reciting a protection prayer: "In the Name of Allah with whose name nothing on earth or in heaven can cause any harm, and He is the all-hearing and all-knowing." When the demonstration was over, they all fastened their seatbelts.

The flight attendant announced the availability of WIFI connectivity on the plane. Um Obied clapped her hands enthusiastically, shouting, "Way to go, Emirates Airlines, a provider of five-star services."

Nora raised her phone and stared happily at its screen, which illuminated with an incoming text message: "Good morning, my love."

She was quick with her reply. "Good morning to you! I'm flying high in the sky, on my way to London, the city of fog. We have inflight internet access, and I can be online with you till our arrival time."

He texted her, "Arrive safely, my love. You let me know when you arrive, okay?" He often puzzled her with his behavior. Sometimes he made her feel she was the most important thing in his life, his everything, and sometimes he just ignored her for days on end with no calls or messages. She hated her affection towards him as much as she loved him.

She took it upon herself to read the novel, as Um Obied was watching an Arabic movie and the others were asleep. Shaking her head every now then, she was progressing through the novel, thinking that it was underserving of the award, and wondering what the award committee's reasoning or ulterior motives were. It could be because of the erotic content, for the novel was more erotic than could be accepted in her culture, she thought. She cast it aside, as she could not stomach it anymore, and decided to leave it behind in the airplane. The next best thing was watching the Arabic movie that was flickering on the large screen at the front of the cabin, an oldie entitled "Mouths and Rabbits," starring Faten Hamama and Mahmoud Yacine. She watched the movie for some time, then the images started to fade as sleep slowly crept over her, overwhelming her with a comforting peace.

The brightly illuminated screen of her mobile phone awakened her; it was an incoming message from Khalid: "My precious, have you arrived?" She texted her response: "Khalid, my darling, we still have one more hour to go. I'll message you when we arrive." Standing up and stretching, she headed to the bathroom to wash her face, tidy her hair, and smooth down her dress. Um Obied, who did not sleep, followed her; despite being a frequent flier, she still feared airplanes, preferring to stay awake the whole time. The plane started to descend gradually towards Heathrow Airport.

Passing through passport control and collecting their baggage, they soon were in their reserved car on the way to their residence, an hour's drive away. When they reached their apartment building, Nora saw it was exactly what she had asked for, overlooking Hyde Park and close to the Hilton Hotel.

"Thanks, Khoula. The apartment is absolutely wonderful. The view of Hyde Park is really great," Nora said enthusiastically, as she walked from room to room.

"Thank God! So you like it, Nora!" Khoula smiled.

Um Obied, feeling drowsy, was looking for a bed to lay her body on, while Huda was occupied with unpacking the food supply bag, which was loaded with spices, coffee, canned food, and regag bread. Hurriedly, she organized the food in the refrigerator and lit incense in the apartment, mostly for the smell but also to bring positivity to their temporary home. At five p.m., Nora grabbed her handbag and told Huda that she was going for a walk in Hyde Park.

She strolled through the entrance opposite the Hilton, and headed directly towards the nearest café. It was just as Muhanna had described it; the seat she chose looked exactly like she had pictured from their conversations. Sipping on her favorite drink, coffee mocha, she pretended he was there with her, in the chair opposite hers, enchanting her with his words and looks. She indulged in daydreams of her time in Alexandria, reminiscing about its remarkable atmosphere, lively streets, el-Haram Hotel, Adel Emam's 1976 play *A Witness Who Hasn't Seen Anything,* and the unique experience of catching a carriage ride in the evening on the beach to watch the sunset. She finished her coffee, her body still feeling strained and tired from the long hours of flight. She left Hyde Park and went to a nearby shopping area to buy weekly bus passes for the whole group. London was famous for its busses, which outnumbered cars as an elegant transportation means throughout the city's many districts; and she greatly preferred the busses over the metro. By the time she returned to the apartment, Um Obied and Khoula had already roused from their snooze, looking completely refreshed.

"Where have you been, Nora?" inquired Huda.

"No place in particular. I had a cup of coffee at Hyde Park and bought us bus passes."

"I don't know how to use the bus," Huda admitted.

"Looks like you forgot our mother's advice, Huda," Nora teased. "She used to say, 'always seek to learn, never say I do not know.' Right?"

"Sure thing," Khoula broke in with a laugh. "Do you remember that story Mother used to tell us when we were little? Our grandfather was an important dignitary in the city. One day, the wife of the British Political Agent invited Sharjah's elite society ladies, including Grandmother, to a tea party. Our mother, who was almost fourteen at the time, accompanied her. The tea was served to them in china cups with saucers, and Mother felt embarrassed, not knowing what to do with the saucer and how to drink her tea. But Grandmother, being clever and wise, told her to wait and watch attentively how the other ladies acted, and then do what they did. She told her not to hurry, and never say you don't know."

"Right, Khoula," Nora agreed. "I learned this wisdom from Mom. I always try to learn new things. Using the public bus system to get around the city is not difficult, for each bus has a number and in each station there is a map that shows the bus routes. You all are familiar with London's roads and districts since you were young, thanks to Monopoly, which made us memorize most of its major and famous roads."

"I'm Um Obied, clever and daring," Um Obied boasted. "I know almost all of London's major roads and areas. Tomorrow morning, I will take the bus and go to Oxford Street."

"Um Obied, bus number 94 takes you to Oxford Street."

"Thank you, my darling Nora. Also, it is cheaper to use the bus. The cost of one trip in a taxi is equal to the cost of using the bus for a full week."

"You're right, Um Obied," Nora said. "But please excuse me, I want to go to my room and rest for a while. Later, we will discuss our dinner plans."

In her room, she checked her mobile phone, but there were no messages from him. A flurry of worrisome questions besieged her. *Why does this man torment me? He was the one who asked to be notified immediately upon my arrival. I have sent him a message and he did not reply. What is wrong with him? I know him well; he will find some excuse to justify his silence.* Her heart stood still in terror as she checked her Twitter account, for it was all aflutter with news of a suicide bomber who set himself off at a Shia grand mosque in Kuwait during Friday prayer, killing twenty-seven people and wounding 227 others. "There's neither power nor ability save by Allah Almighty—why do you target the worshippers and shed the blood of innocent people? First in Saudi Arabia and today in Kuwait. What is it you want? What's wrong with you?"

She ran out back into the living room. "Turn on the TV! There is a suicide bombing attack on a mosque in Kuwait. May Allah take revenge on them for killing worshippers in mosques. May Allah make their evil backfire on them!"

"Amen," they all concurred.

Nora burst into a crying jag, watching the limbs and body parts of victims strewn throughout the area of the blast, hearing the wails of the wounded people, and the sobs of families mourning their loved ones. At that instant, she suddenly remembered her lover. Hurriedly she sent him a message: "Please let me know you're all right."

Her joy and relief were overwhelming when he wrote her back. "Thank Allah, my love, I'm fine. I'm sure you heard the terrible news. I'm now on duty twenty-four hours a day. Don't think too much, and try to take care of yourself. I'll call you at the nearest opportunity. Make sure to have a good time, and don't forget to pass by the café I told you about, and sit on the same chair I did."

Um Obied and Huda were busy preparing lunch, Khoula was on her mobile phone, and Omar was still in bed. Setting the table, Um Obied said boastfully, "I have cooked Tuna Makbus for you, Nora—it's so delicious that you will lick your fingers over it."

"I truly lost my appetite, Um Obied, when I heard the news of what's happening in our region," she said.

"May Allah help us and protect our region and countries from all kinds of harm. But we all ought to eat now. Then we can go out walking on Edgware Road—it's a good time as the weather is nice, and no one would question four Gulf Arab ladies taking a walk."

"You're right, Um Obied," Nora said. "It's really a good time for walking and we should seize the moment, but I don't like Edgware Road."

"Then Khoula and Huda and I will take the bus there," Um Obied said. "Perhaps you'd rather walk somewhere else."

"God speed. I will walk around Hyde Park and Oxford Street," Nora replied, and started gathering the table scraps and breadcrumbs in a plastic bag to feed the birds in Hyde Park.

She went through the same entrance as the day before, sat on the same chair, ordered her coffee, and drifted away into daydreams. She was not interested in anything around her in the park. His face floated through her thoughts, making her unable to see the faces of other people around her or care about them. She only returned the greetings of Gulf Arab visitors who passed her by. Today she ordered chocolate ice cream instead of her favorite coffee and ate it in silence, tears streaming down her face.

Feeling down and distressed since he had not called her for days, she distracted herself by reading a novel entitled *The Bamboo Stalk*, winner of the International Prize for Arabic Fiction and written by Saud Alsanousi, a young Kuwaiti novelist. She was captivated by the novel's honesty, scope, and depiction of the issues associated with migration and rootlessness. It told the story of a half-Filipino, half-Kuwaiti teen moving from an underprivileged life in the Philippines to a life in the promised "paradise," his father's country, Kuwait. Her heart literally ached over the fate of the novel's hero, thinking of how the novel actually mirrored the dilemma of the Gulf society's house servants.

The days passed on and Nora did the same things—dining with her sisters, browsing a shop or two, and then returning to the same seat in Hyde Park. Whenever she came back to the apartment, she would find her sisters proudly going over their innumerable purchases from London's outlets. Nora's focus really wasn't on shopping, but she did buy perfumes and designer bags for herself and Alia, and picked up some small gifts for her friend Salma, who called every day asking about the ever present/absent lover.

One day Nora wrote a message to him: "I wish you would come to London so we could sit together here in our coffee shop, even for just few moments."

"You know the situation in the Gulf. I could not get time off from work," he responded.

"I need you. I need to talk with you. I don't know why, but I really need you right now. Why don't you answer my calls?"

"You've become a little insistent, my love. Please understand that I have commitments. I have my work and my family to take care of."

"Please don't blame me for asking," she replied. "I don't know how I lived through the past twenty-six years without you. I've grown more and more addicted to patience until my heart bleeds. But now I can't bear being away from you any longer."

She turned off her mobile phone and began walking towards the lake to feed the birds and ducks the leftover bread she brought along. Then, she went back again to the coffee shop, deciding to continue reading the novel over a cup of mocha coffee. To her surprise, there was a handsome Gulf Arab sitting in her seat.

She immediately felt enraged. She held her anger in check but nonetheless thought to herself, *That is my seat, mine. How could that Gulf Arab do such thing?* However, upon seeing her, the man swiftly stood up and walked away, leaving behind a small piece of paper on the table. She hurried to her seat, took the folded paper, and read it.

"'If a lady turns to you, you need to listen to her and be willing to die for her, since a lady only turns to a real man.' I read this line on Twitter and liked it very much, so I thought of sharing it with you, because somehow I think it relates to you. Every day, I see you sitting here, tears rolling down your pretty face. Is he worth your tears and pain? It hurts to see your beautiful eyes saddened by human affairs."

She hadn't had the opportunity to observe his features. She put the paper in her handbag, with a vague question as to who he might be, wondering why she did not take notice of him during the past days while he was able to see right through her and understand more than she wanted anyone to know.

She made her way to the bus station, and rode bus 74, which took her directly to Harrods, the world's most famous department store. She brought out her phone and earphone and clicked a link that Muhanna had sent her; it was a song, one of his favorites, by the singer Angham. She sang silently along, "For the love of God, please go and leave me with him; I won't take long—I just want to spend my life with him."

The voice of the bus driver pulled her back to the real world; he had just ordered her to get off the bus as it had reached the end of its route. She realized that she was the only one on the bus. She got off, hesitating a little, but soon she was able to recognize that she was in the Cromwell District and the Emirates airline office was just further down the road. She crossed the road to catch the return bus, debating in her mind whether to return to the apartment or push on with her plan to shop at Harrods.

In the bus, she began blaming herself; her emotions must be very transparent if the man at the coffee shop was able to read the signs of pain and sorrow on her face and see her soul.

"What a failure I am!" Nora murmured to herself bitterly. "Why has this happened to me when I am the one who always stayed strong in the face of troubles, the one that crowds of grown people listen to as I lecture in major cities? May Allah grant you forgiveness, Muhanna! Why can't you see what I have done for you?"

She alighted from the bus on Oxford Street. Then, out of nowhere and for no apparent reason, the idea popped into her mind to go to Madame Tussaud's, so she boarded bus 20. She walked into the museum, pushing through crowds of people. She stared in awe at the wax model of the Indian actor Shahrukh Khan, recalling the famous line he always used to say in his movies: "I'm certain you love me." Muhanna seemed certain of that as well. But did he love her the same?

She stopped at the figure of Queen Elizabeth II and took a photo with it. She liked the sculptures of Benazir Bhutto and the Iron Lady, Margaret Thatcher. She was enjoying herself but felt all alone in the crowd. Deep inside, she wanted to be like everyone else around, those couples with families and loving gazes. She wished he could be there with her at that moment, yet she knew that her wishes were playing hard to get.

It was late by the time she finished her tour in the company of her thoughts and imagination. As she was getting ready to leave, Khoula called.

"Where are you, Nora? I'm really worried about you."

"Don't be worried, darling. I know London very well. I'm at the wax museum right now. What about you?"

"We're in Shepherd's Bush, because Huda wants to buy some cotton robes for her friends. And we'll probably have falafel here—they make it so well."

"Fine. As soon as I'm done with my tour, I'll head right back to the apartment. I'll stop for some fish and chips on my way."

At the bus station, she boarded bus 20 back to Oxford Street where she could catch bus 94 to Queensway. Salma sent her a link to her favorite song, *My Love*, by the Mauritanian singer Malouma Bint El Meidah. Normally, she was not a big fan of that style of music, yet she felt confused and could not comprehend the changes in herself, as if she were going through a midlife crisis. Her life felt in disarray when he came back to her, although he had always been on her mind and in her heart. She recalled the time when he put the phone on speaker mode for her to hear, and told his daughter-in-law, "My friend finally found his sweetheart after twenty-six years of searching."

"Oh my God, this is a great love story! They should get together right away," a female voice replied.

She got off at her station. Knowing that her sisters were eating at Shepherd's Bush, she stopped for fish and chips. In the apartment, she lay down on her bed, closing her eyelids tightly and hoping to drift off to sleep and leave all her worries behind. But she found herself wide-eyed and awake when she remembered her plan to visit Al Saqi Bookshop, just few blocks away, to buy some literary books. She blamed herself for forgetting the plan. Was it too late to go now? The comfort of her warm bed influenced her decision to postpone the visit until tomorrow, since she was committed to visiting Hyde Park in the evening as a daily habit.

She was in a deep sleep, after a long tiring day spent walking in the wax museum. Suddenly, she woke up to the voice of Um Obied.

"My head is about to burst—I'm seriously in need of some Arabic coffee. Khoula, please make us some!"

Nora wandered into the living room. "Wow, looks like you went on a shopping spree. You bought almost everything in sight at the marketplace, you shopping addicts!" she exclaimed.

"Pretty much. What about you, Nora?"

"I don't buy just anything and everything, and I certainly don't buy for the sake of buying!" Nora answered. "By the way, I'm going to Bicester Village to do some shopping tomorrow. If any of you would like to come along, please know that we must leave at eight in the morning. We'll take the train from Marylebone Station because tomorrow is Monday, and there will be less traffic."

"I'll go with you!" Khoula bubbled with enthusiasm. "I want to buy some designer bags for my daughters Muhra and Meera."

"All right, Khoula, just be ready at eight."

"Me too!" Um Obied interrupted. "I want to go with you!"

"Sure thing, Um Obied. Try to go to bed early, and be ready for tomorrow. Please excuse me now—I'm going out to walk around in Hyde Park."

As she walked, she realized a week had passed without any calls or messages from him. She remembered the letter she found on her table at the café, and decided to read it again, wondering who the man might be and why he cared about her. Replacing the letter in her bag, she entered the park and headed to her usual seat at the café, ordered her usual coffee, and lost herself in the memories of Alexandria and its lively streetscape. Her mobile phone rang, snapping her back to reality; it was Khoula.

"Nora, I have surprising news for you—you won't believe me if I told you."

"Khoula, please, you know I can't handle surprises."

"Guess who's sitting next to me on the bus. It's someone you love."

Her heart leapt into her throat. Could it be—? But no, of course not. Khoula didn't know him. "Please, Khoula, tell me now."

"Calm down, Nora. It's Aunt Samira—remember her?"

"How could I forget her! How, where?"

"Here, talk to her."

A familiar voice came on the line. "Hello, Nora."

"Aunt Samira, it's been twenty-two years since we last heard from you, when you suddenly moved to Bahrain. Oh, God, what an amazing coincidence. Do you have kids of your own?"

"Yes," said Aunt Samira. "My eldest is a girl—I named her Nora, after you. I'm here in London to attend her graduation ceremony from medical school. I also have two sons, Abdullah and Ahmad, who are in high school."

"How happy I am to hear this! You must come and see us, for I missed you so much. Please bring your Nora with you as well."

"I will, sweetheart. I will pass by your hotel the day after tomorrow. You must promise me to attend my daughter's graduation ceremony this Thursday, all right?"

"God, I miss you so much!" Nora said, overcome with happiness. "I want to know everything about you—tell me all the little details."

Aunt Samira laughed lightly. "Exactly the same—our eager, impetuous Nora! I'll fill you in when I see you! And you must fill me in, too."

As the call ended, the memory of her wedding day surfaced in her mind. Feeling very helpless, just hours before the party, she had run to Aunt Samira's house, laid her head down in her auntie's lap and cried with all her heart as she bared her soul to her. Would she now bare her soul again to her, telling her that he had once more appeared in her life after so many long years, tormenting her?

Whenever his image filled her mind, her body would come alive, she would lose control of herself, and tears would stream down her face. She snapped back to reality at the sight of someone standing before her.

"Can I sit with you, my princess?" the man asked.

She tried to hide the tears that rolled from her eyes, down her cheeks, and onto her dress. She recognized him; it was the same man who had left her a note in Hyde Park.

"Yes, by all means. Have we been introduced before? Do you know me?"

"I wrote a letter to you," he said with a smile, seating himself across from her. "For two weeks now, I always find you sitting in the same place, your eyes glowing with tears, the sound of your weeping breaking my heart. I asked myself 'Why would these beautiful eyes cry?' I couldn't bear it anymore, so I wrote a letter to you yesterday, and you took it. I'm sure you must have read it."

"Yes, of course, I read it. It was nice of you. I think you're from the Gulf region, but I'm not sure from which country you are."

"I'm Qatari, from Doha," revealed the man.

"Thank you for your gentle letter. Sometimes worries and concerns are more than a person can bear, and crying helps in wiping away the worries and reducing the stress. But not all worries and concerns are related to love, as you might have imagined."

"I want to apologize for my intrusion into your private life, but seeing you sitting alone, looking heartbroken, compelled me to write the letter. Once again, my apologies. But please level with me—it's a man who caused you to be unhappy, right?"

"Well, yes, it's a man, just so you have a peace of mind," she sighed.

"Thank you for your candidness. I'm very proud of you," said the man with sincerity in his voice. "As a well-educated person, tactful in your speech and manners, and modest in your dress, still you remained faithful to wearing the abaya, even here in the middle of London. Unfortunately, a lot of Gulf women travel to Europe, while leaving their culture, values, customs, and traditions behind. The first time I saw you, I felt that you're a very respectable lady. But seeing your eyes welling up with tears, and your face drooping with sadness, made my heart bleed. So I thought of writing to you, hoping to ease your pain and lighten your life. I ask you to look on me as a brother and a friend. This is my number—you can call me anytime, should you need anything."

"Thank you, my dear brother. I'm honored to have a friend like you. Please forgive me, I must go back home now as night is about to fall. I hope to see you again."

She left the coffee shop and went directly to the apartment, aiming to sleep early in readiness for a full day trip to Bicester Village in the morning. In order to get there, they would need to change two buses to reach Marylebone Station, then take the train to their destination.

She tried to sleep, but his image was burned into her eyelids, although he had not been in touch with her for a week now. She scrolled her mobile phone, going through the old WhatsApp voice messages he had sent her before, unconsciously closing her eyes, letting his gentle voice charm her to sleep. Still, she lay awake most of the night, tossing and turning, thoughts and questions churning through her mind: Muhanna's face, the Qatari man who fascinated her with his gentleness, and her desire to meet Aunt Samira and know more about her Pakistani husband. Was Samira still married to him or did she leave him for another? She tightly closed her eyes, recited the Verses of Refuge from the Quran, and counted praise and blessings until sleep claimed her.

She rose to the sound of a loud knock on the door. It was Um Obied, who took it upon herself to wake the travelers up every day.

"Nora, Khoula, Huda, I have made breakfast for you. It's already seven o'clock. We have to catch the 8:30 train so we can get back here at five in the evening."

She sprang up, hurriedly changed her clothes, and sat at the dining table. "May Allah bless you, Um Obied my darling, for this high-class breakfast. Come on, everyone, we have a train to catch," she chortled in joy.

Most of the people on the train were vacationers and shoppers from the Gulf region. She quietly settled in a window seat, watching the landscape glide by. Khoula, Huda, and Um Obied engrossed themselves in conversation. They were supposed to get off at the third station, but Nora, deeply absorbed in her thoughts and the beautiful scenery outside her window, was oblivious to the passage of time and surroundings. Realizing what had happened too late, after the train had already moved, she shouted, "Khoula, Um Obied, Huda, we missed our station! We were supposed to get off at the last stop. You got carried away in your conversation and excitement."

"*We* got carried away?" Khoula asked. "We were depending on you, Nora!"

"But you know English pretty well. You must have noticed our fellow Gulf Arabs getting off when the train stopped, so why didn't you just follow suit? Come on now, get ready," she commanded. "We should get off at the next station, then take the return train back to our stop. From there, we will take the bus."

It was such a long day, but they all returned with some purchases, taking advantage of the greatly discounted prices at outlet stores. The whole time, her mind was preoccupied with tomorrow's meeting with Aunt Samira. Overwhelmed with anxiety and anticipation, she kept checking her mobile phone, hoping to receive a message from him, asking herself why he had become hard-hearted and unjust to her again—hadn't she had enough of that all these years? Unable to curb her growing impatience, she texted him: "What a cruel man you are! I have asked for nothing but simply to see you or hear from you."

She turned off her mobile phone and went to sleep, hoping to wake up rested and relaxed for her meeting with Aunt Samira. She wanted to hear her news, but even more, she wanted to tell her about the lover who showed up after many years to torture her yet again. He broke her heart once before, and now he was going to break what was left of her soul.

First thing in the morning, she grabbed her mobile phone and scrolled through the new messages. A soft gasp escaped her as she saw Muhanna's message among them. Finally, he had found it in his heart to write. "You're unjust to me. What else could I have done? Have you a suggestion?"

The doorbell rang, and she ran to answer it; there on the threshold stood Aunt Samira. Hugging her tight in her arms, Nora cried, "Is this real or a dream? After all these years, where have you been? Come in, let me look at you. Please stay with us tonight—I want to stay up all night with you and tell you everything, and hear everything about you. Tell me about your husband Abdulhameed—how is he and how is he doing? You left us without a word. What made you leave the country all of a sudden?"

"Thank Allah, we're all fine and well. You knew about my estrangement from my family. Six years after I married, I became pregnant with my little girl, Nora. Then my father called me, and through his tears asked me to return to Bahrain, saying he has forgiven me for everything and that he needed me. I couldn't believe my ears, you know. He missed me, because he was growing old."

"So you returned! How did your father receive you, with open arms?"

"Yes, Nora. You can't imagine the longing I had to see him. I will never forget that moment and the tears of my father as he kissed my hands and I kissed his feet, washing them with my tears, asking him to forgive me. Life away from the homeland is very tough, Nora."

"And what about your husband, Abdulhameed?"

"He returned with me, of course, and went back to working with my father again, hand in hand, as if he were his son. My father later helped him become a citizen of Bahrain. And what about you? Tell me everything about your life."

"Thank Allah, my daughter Alia just got married a month ago, and my son Khalid has graduated from college."

"That's great. And you, how are you doing?"

"I'm alive! You know, even though I had not seen him or heard from him in years, the man I loved never left my mind since the day we met. But he appeared again in my life two months ago—he searched for me and found me. We then exchanged messages only, with no plan for a meet-up. Sadly, though, his messages stopped coming a few days ago—he said it wasn't right for us to meet or exchange messages since we have our families to care for. I'm exhausted by all this, but I still love him."

"Oh Nora, my heart goes out to you. It seems that no solution is in sight, but you two must meet together and talk. This might provide you with peace and comfort. You're a media personality—you normally meet with colleagues and lecture students—so why not have an innocent meeting with him?" suggested Aunt Samira.

"I truly don't know. I asked him to meet up but he didn't oblige. I pray to Allah to grant me strength and patience and to let me forget him, for I've grown so very tired. Please forgive me—I made you stay up late into the night. But it is so good to talk to someone who understands."

The next day, Nora took the bus to Piccadilly Street, remembering to buy a few things that her children needed. After she had done all her shopping, she spent some time at Piccadilly Circus, looking around and gleefully watching some acrobatic street performers. Her mobile phone rang; the screen showed a Kuwaiti number.

"Hello?" Her heart was thudding painfully, and she was momentarily thunderstruck.

"Where are you, my love?" Muhanna said.

"I'm at Piccadilly Circus, watching some street acts, hoping to forget my pain and heartbreak. Then I plan to go to Selfridges Department Store to have lunch with my sisters."

As she turned her head to cross the street, she gasped in surprise and the mobile phone fell from her hand. There he was, standing right in front of her! She found herself looking at him as she never had before, noting how the years had touched him. She knew she had changed over the years as well, and was no longer the girl he had last seen a quarter of a century ago. The encounter made her speechless, the words she wished to say to him hung on the tip of her tongue, but not a word escaped her lips. He too was wordless, staring at her face.

A long, silent moment passed between them, broken when her mobile phone rang. Muhanna reached down to pick up the phone from the ground, just as he had picked up her passport a lifetime before. He handed the phone to Nora and she saw the caller was her husband, Eisa.

She looked up at Muhanna. “I can’t,” she whispered. “It’s over. I’m done.”

Then she answered the phone call. “Hey, Abu Khalid.” It was hard to speak; she cleared her throat. “We’re flying back early in the morning, at dawn. Are you going to pick us up at the airport?”

“Sure. I really missed you, Um Khalid.”

She halted when she realized that she was walking inside Selfridges without knowing how she reached there—whether she walked all the way there or managed to take a bus. Was the man she just saw a few minutes ago real or solely a figment of her overheated imagination?

Either way, she knew that part of her life was over. She had to get on with the rest.

THE END

About the Translator

Abdallah Altaiyeb is a novelist, short story writer, poet, essayist, and translator. He was born and raised in Medina on the west coast of Saudi Arabia. He studied chemical engineering, earned both MBA and DBA degrees, and worked as a manager for the national oil company, Saudi Aramco. His first translated anthology, *On the Weave of the Sun*, published in 2012, was called an exhilarating treasure chest of short stories that resonated with readers everywhere and presented great Arabic literature to the world. In 2019, he published his second translated anthology, entitled *Ascension on the Wings of a Tale*, featuring works of fifty talented Arab writers. He has also published a novel and several articles in peer-reviewed journals. His email address is altaiyeb@live.com.

Review Requested:

If you loved this book, would you please provide a review at Amazon.com?

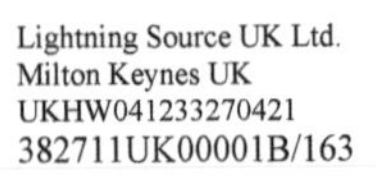

Lightning Source UK Ltd.
Milton Keynes UK
UKHW041233270421
382711UK00001B/163